Jack Frusciante

Has Left the Band

Jack Frusciante Has Left the Band

A Love Story—with Rock 'n' Roll

Enrico Brizzi

Translated from the Italian by Stash Luczkiw

Grove Press
New York

First published in Italy by Baldini & Castoldi.

Published simultaneously in Canada
Printed in the United States of America

FIRST AMERICAN EDITION

Library of Congress Cataloging-in-Publication Data

Brizzi, Enrico, 1974-
    [Jack Frusciante è uscito dal gruppo. English]
    Jack Frusciante has left the band : a love story—with rock 'n'
roll / Enrico Brizzi ; translated from the Italian by Stash Luczkiw.
        p.   cm.
    ISBN 0-8021-3521-8
    I. Luczkiw, Stash.   II. Title.
    PQ4862.R5717J3313   1997
    853'.914—dc21   97-25065
                                                           CIP

DESIGN BY LAURA HAMMOND HOUGH

Grove Press
841 Broadway
New York, NY 10003

97 98 99 00 10 9 8 7 6 5 4 3 2 1

For Andrea P. and T.
who drew and wrote

Jack Frusciante

Has Left the Band

Intro

soon even that stupid
February would've flown away

soon even that stupid February would've flown away and Alex felt terribly unhappy, but in a detached way, as if his life belonged to someone else, a raw feeling—all too typical, I admit

no need to sneer though, because by that time Alex hadn't even turned eighteen, and in those days the Bologna sky was about as eloquent as a deaf block of cast iron, and you couldn't've expected much from a sky like that, not even one of those beautiful storms—the kind that washes the streets once and for all after nearly two weeks under a pallid nameless rain, and rouses the city from its catatonic state

as someone who knows Alex and the facts of his life I'll limit myself to saying that a certain girl he'd been hanging out with was already fading from his memory, crumpled by the staggering squalor of daily life: the fact that he'd been so happy with her for four months seemed meaningless—another one of his harshest feelings

it's like this: till he was sixteen and a half our prim, proper and absolutely-full-of-goodwill youngster was left to rot a hair's breadth from the teacher's desk where he would diligently take notes, the sweetheart, so helpful! so dedicated! a regular brownnosing cadaver of bookishness, the kind of student who *never* skulked in late, seeing as how his Alsatian guilt complex would've ended up killing him otherwise, and cutting class? you must be kidding

believe me, he was breathtakingly devoted, that is until early one morning in May, just before dawn, after finishing *Two out of Two* by Andrea De Carlo, the madman decided with a youthful, feverish and apparently superhuman firmness that nothing would be like it'd been before, that thanks to *Two out of Two* his eyes'd been opened to all the useless bullshit around him: like irregular verb tables, summary outlines, the school board's phony democracy, the mindless conformity of his peers and the teachers' two-faced way of paying lip service to the sanctity of independent judgment while punishing the slightest sign of autonomy with a subtle rage, those bastards

in September, at the beginning of his fourth year, old Alex was redeemed and he and his friend Oscar could be seen dashing up the stairs ahead of a sleepwalking group of students to take seats in the lecture hall's back corner, darting around like young dogs getting into their new roles as do-nothings and troublemakers, and so the fall and winter just blew by, slow and numb between the yellowish walls of Liceo Caimani, but it was all electric and speed away from the jail, *outside,* in the company of Depression Tony and Helios Nardini and old Hoge of the phosphorescent skull, the only guy in the world who believed (I swear it took months to convince the guy he was wrong) that the correct spelling of blue jeans was blujinx

by the beginning of March the good weather was already beaming through the city, and every morning God would unroll one of those blue skies with a few white cotton-puff clouds suspended in the distance and it was impossible not to giggle out of happiness or step out onto the balcony or go out into the street and resist the temptation to shout: thanks, chief, I won't forget it!

old Alex would brush his teeth three times a day and go to school to warm his bench and write "principal shithead" and "filthy rot-aryan assholes" on the bathroom doors, and then would go back home and eat spaghetti, veal cutlets and apples in a hurry, improve his Tetris record, and then in no time would bolt again, riding his bike headlong into via Saragozza and stay out till late in the afternoon because at that point the Matron was totally fed up with throwing all his good-for-nothingness in his face and had already written her darling little boy off

Alex loved the cobblestones of via Collegio di Spangna, the quick asphalt of the alleys, the stretch of porphyry along via Rizzoli, and all the rest, the orange sunsets behind San Luca's, wearing a new T-shirt, going up to see Grandma Pina for a snack at her place and ranting about politics or TV

sweet Adelaide was still in town essentially . . .

you see, there'd been afternoons when old Alex desired Adelaide with such a rage it could've hurt him, but he held back, not even just . . .

you'll see.

so between all the missed innuendos, after all the longing and throbbing, she wound up studying in America for a year thanks to one of those nutty cultural exchanges and registered with some association which made her pass loads of aptitude tests and then the English test and then, of course, some payments, and after getting through all this stuff she got a typed letter in the mail from three nice, solid and open Pennsylvanians: father, mother and fifteen-year-old son—a middle-friggin-class family embedded in domestic walls where there would always be plenty of room for fun after work, provided it was good-clean-healthy fun

during her stay there Alex wrote once in a while and Adelaide also wrote him and once she even called—it was five in the morning on via Saragozza and she was crying

(he'd never loved like he did now)

meanwhile, the cast-iron sky continued to reign over the city and Adelaide had already been gone some weeks

(maybe one really loves only in memory—or so it's been written) anyway, all Alex could do was feel deeply unhappy, but in a detached way, and try to remember what they'd had together: he kept thinking it over, writing about it even though everything got all tangled up and he couldn't find the words and wound up seeing only details and that's it: meeting with her in front of Feltrinelli's bookstore, a little word from her, always from her, with that special smile and runaway gaze

his whole life till then could've fit into his Jollinvicta backpack.

Adelaide had left in early summer and now it was mid-February—a wretched February that crept along the walls of via Porrettana like a Sunday rain dog—and all Alex could feel was this useless little pain in the pit of his soul.

* * *

(then one afternoon more dazed and confused than the others, our old boy thought about how those stories of dogs that could bring newspapers to their masters were a load of egregious bull, and in fact he'd never even seen such a feat, and in any case it would've slobbered all over the paper)

all right all right, sure . . .

one step at a time—yessir . . .

okay let's start this splotchy story from the top and

think it through, yes.

ONE

That pseudospringlike

Sunday afternoon

That pseudospringlike Sunday afternoon, while scrambling up the stairs, Alex had a premonition, or better yet, a *telephoto* premonition. He could see his family barricaded in the living room, watching some American crap on video. An instant later, before he even slipped off his parka, he realized that these chillingly realistic telephotos showed him to what extent his faculties of clairvoyance had, with age, reached astoundingly necromantic proportions. They were *all* in the living room, each one engrossed in or appalled by the rough-and-tumble scenes in *Rocky IV. Frère de lait* was sucked into the action, already dreaming of becoming a pro boxer. The Matron seesawed dangerously between the images on the screen and the Bologna metro section in *La Repubblica.* The Chancellor, half swallowed up by the armchair and smiling for no reason, accompanied midget Stallone's uppercuts with depressing imitations of Ivan Drago's robotic voice and one-liners spat out by a faltering nervous system.

"Jesus," Alex muttered to himself, suddenly feeling his strength wane. "Weren't these poor souls a living Italian family light-years ago?" You could hardly believe it. But shit, even if his heart and mind *were* devoured by disbelief, it still didn't keep him from taking his turn seated in front of the idiot box.

Okay, the radioactive TV screen was beaming the muscle-bound dwarf's brawny epic—there could be no doubts, we're

6

not talking trailer here, they were showing the *whole* movie. Just then, as the dire and maybe final menace from the Soviet robot Drago was hovering over little Stallone, the phone rang. Now I won't disrespect you all by omitting the fact that if Alex had only even distantly imagined how through those rings sweet Adelaide was just about to burst into his life, he would've hardly answered it with such a foot-dragging who-gives-a-shit attitude, but would've donned a multicolored feather suit and a pair of solid gold shoes instead.

"Hello?" he kept himself to saying, though with a magnificent baritone and phonogenic timbre granted him by a devastating puberty.

"Is this the D. residence?"

"Yes, it is," old Alex acknowledged.

"I'd like to speak with Alessandro, please. I'm one of his schoolmates."

"Speaking," said our old boy, poising himself in expectation.

"Oh, hi. Listen, I'm Adelaide," answered the voice at the other end of the line. "Francesca's friend. You know, third year?"

Sure. He made the connection: Francesca was a cute babe from school; in fact they'd been seeing each other for twenty days some time back, and Adelaide, who came from Sicily, was her best friend. What else did he know? Oh yeah, that she'd been hanging out with Federico Laterza, a feral beast in Gore-Tex who our old boy couldn't stomach and who had a surprisingly cute older sister. The older sister had finished high school the year before. She was in Federico Laterza's class, and by now they were both swirling through the swiss-cheese world of university. Francesca had always said good things about Adelaide. They were really close friends.

Old Alex even talked to her once.

About poetry among other things.

"Hi," he said. It didn't come out as enthusiastically as he would've liked, but he knew everyone behind the barricade had their ears pricked up, and this didn't make his live performance any easier. "How's it going?"

"Good, thanks. And you?"

"Average." That's what he always said.

"Out of it?" Communication breakdown.

"*Average,*" he repeated. "Nothing real bad, but nothing to get excited over." He knew the Chancellor was now smiling sardonically.

"Oh, *average*. Listen, Alex, you remember when we had that conversation about cummings, that incredible poet I was telling you about?"

"cummings? You bet!" he told her. "Of course I remember."

cummings, it was the only thing they'd ever talked about. They talked about poets as life models, as myths, as crowbars to pry open the mediocrity of everyday life and fly a kite in the meadow beyond. She was into cummings; and old Alex was into that massive skull of Baudelaire. He didn't know what cummings did in life, but she talked about him like he was some genius and promised she would lend him his complete works to read, or whatever.

"That book I was telling you about, the collection . . . I mean, I have it, I can bring it to you."

"Incredible," Alex said to himself, gripping the receiver with two hands. "Christ." He felt several inches taller. "Yeah, we could do that," he told her. He decided to take his time so as not to seem too anxious.

"Good old cummings." He sighed. "Why don't we see each other later? Maybe in *half an hour*? Do you have time, in half an hour?"

"All right," she answered.

"So I'll meet you in half an hour then, downtown?"

"All right. I'll bring the book."

"Christ," old Alex said to himself. He checked his watch with the most tigerlike expression he could muster and said: "It's about quarter to four now. How about we meet at four fifteen, four twenty in front of Feltrinelli's?"

"Four twenty sounds good."

"In front of Feltrinelli's," he repeated, to be sure there was no doubt. "Under the two towers."

"By the two towers," said the voice at the other end of the line.

"Right." Alex gave it a thought. "See you there in half an hour." He felt the palms of his hands go damp and senseless. He waited for her to hang up, then checked his watch again. "Christ," he said to himself, his eyes shining a conspicuous light mixed with extraordinary hope.

He crossed the living room with his tigerlike expression and said: "I'm gonna hop over to Feltrinelli's."

The pumped-up midget on the screen was running for his life across an expanse of snow in Wyoming or someplace like that.

"Feltrinelli's is *closed*," the Chancellor commented from his armchair.

"I don't have to go in the bookstore," he said. "I'm meeting someone *in front.*"

"How's that?" the Matron interjected without peeling her eyes off the metro section. "You just got in, and now you're leaving already?"

"I told you, I gotta meet someone."

"Meet who?"

"A friend from school, just some girl."

"Some girl? What does that mean?"

"You don't know her. What difference does it make if I tell you her name? You don't know her anyway."

"What's her name?" she insisted. "Did you study enough for tomorrow?"

Self-control. Test of will, test of will. "Yes, I studied. I'll go over it tonight if I have to. Her name is *Adelaide,* all right?"

"Adelaide. And what time are you coming back?"

Test of will, test of will. "I'll be back for dinner, okay?"

"Chancellor, did you hear? The little prince wants to be back for dinner . . . Listen, do you think you live in a hotel, is that it?"

"You tell me what time then," old Alex replied, slipping into his parka. "In any case, no, I don't think I live in a hotel. I just have to meet someone at Feltrinelli's."

"What would seem like a decent time to you?" the Chancellor asked, continuing to plunge imperceptibly into the armchair.

Test of will, test of will. "Is it all right if I come back at seven?"

"Is that all right, Fran?" The Matron's name was Fran.

"You think we're all little idiots, don't you? You think you can lord over us," she said.

All right.

"Anyway, just go."

All right.

"But the point isn't going out or not *today,* the point is that you stay here only as long as it suits you."

Test of will. If you raise your voice they might wind up grounding you. "Six thirty seems more than reasonable to me," Alex said, summoning all the diplomatic resources available to him from the chthonic depths of his parka.

At that point, *Frère de lait,* recovering for a split second from one of his preadolescent and rigorously asexual torpors, though still visibly in the flux of *Rocky IV,* said: "Where are you off to?"

"He's going out, poor kid," the barricade leader remarked ironically. "He's going back *out* because it *bores* him here."

If old Alex pedaled with the desperate energy of a slightly shorter and grungier Girardengo, the great cycling champion, it wasn't just because he had a rendezvous, but because he wanted to get away from the ringside. In any case, he was about to meet Adelaide, and the madman pedaled furiously, like no one else, and sang "White Man in Hammersmith Palais" with a deep, out of tune voice as he pedaled.

Old Alex. If he'd known the kind of musical he was getting into, he would've never started things off with that stupid cowboy shuffle and out of tune Sunday face of his when he got off the bike . . .

Adelaide's little white scooter was already parked. She was in front of Feltrinelli's, looking at the book covers in the window, wearing a green sweater and a zen smile—impenetrable, but very understanding.

No, if Alex'd had the slightest inkling of the kind of musical he was getting himself into, he wouldn't've shown up with that usual mug of his. Instead he would've pulled one of those sinister grins à la Nicholson or De Niro out of his top hat, or at least something ice cool, full of urgency, like Swan in *Warriors*. In the end he came out with "Uh, hi," half-kneeling against his bike, busy with the bike chain. He breathed with his mouth wide open and that damn chain in his hand. "So, how're we doin'?" he said in a somewhat strangled tone.

They walked downtown. Both their ages together didn't add up to thirty-three and a half. They started talking about what they'd like to do in Life, how everything up till then seemed a little unreal, easy and fake. Adelaide—Aidi to her friends (I know, I know, it sounds like that girl in the cartoon who lived in a Swiss cottage)—wanted to live in India, but wasn't sure if as a missionary or photographer or.

Alex wanted to be something like a journalist because it was a way of putting two really awesome things together, traveling and writing. "I want to be a reporter," he told her, terribly serious. "Take off for Cuba or Mozambique with a press pass dangling from my Ramones T-shirt. I swear if I become a reporter I'll get a crew cut and some Clarks shoes." Not bad, eh?

Aidi talked about her ex-boyfriends, a couple of relationships that had left her more or less disappointed. But she didn't talk about it in a bitchy way, like I've been with Older Guys than you. And she didn't come off with the other attitude either, like I've never had any Serious Experiences even though I *could* have. No. There was something blinding about her sincerity, every time she said something—*anything*—she managed to create a mist of charm and fascination around her. And you could see for miles she wasn't posing.

"My God," Alex thought, walking next to her. He felt several inches taller beside her and thought, "This is no girl, this is a whole Battisti album."

Once in a while, when they stopped talking, she would smile at him like a winter dawn. "Christ," Alex thought. "My God," he said to himself.

Then it came out that she was supposed to go to America that summer. She'd do her fourth year there, and it was clear that this fact was at the front of her mind. She talked about it like it was the first real test of her life. At one point she called the moment of her departure "the great flight"—nothing wrong with that, right?—but everything she said had something distinctly poetic about it. She liked Bologna, she liked the narrow streets of the old Jewish quarter, by the university, the conservatory and the theater. The same streets old Alex loved.

At one point they took via Zamboni. The weather was already nice that Sunday afternoon, guys holding hands with their girlfriends, riding in cars with their sleeves rolled up.

Along via Zamboni Adelaide asked him in a direct, almost brutal way why he always came off like the pissed-off prince at school. What did he do in the afternoons, did he feel lonely, was he bummed out, what the hell did he do?

Okay. Francesca might not have spoken of him in totally enthusiastic terms. But still, the two of them went to sit on the bench in front of the No to Racism graffiti on the side of the museum.

Could you tell from looking at the blue sky that spring was around the corner? No. I don't think so. Still, *he* could tell. And I swear, whatever image you had of him from the outside, he felt open and spontaneous like never in his life. Alex was the kind of guy who liked to pretend at times. He was into shocking. Maybe he was an asshole now and then; but on that Sunday afternoon he and Aidi talked about things that had been stuffed inside for years so naturally and with such a longing that it was magic: Aidi's paranoia vis-à-vis her separated parents, Alex's fear of his folks considering him just an extension of themselves . . . You understand. It was as if he'd already been there, sitting against the bench's backrest. As if Aidi had already known him. Between the folds of his memory, in the video archive of elementary school, there was something of her: Villa Spada, where he went to play with the cub scouts, lunches at his uncle and aunt's in Casalecchio every Sunday; the blue Renault that the Chancellor had bought when Alex was six; the bathroom mirror with a halo of condensation on which *Frère de lait* wrote "Inter-Milan #1"; and then certain distorted riffs from a Fender Jaguar in his mind . . . Anyway, there was something of her in all that, and old Alex managed to be more than nice and more than natural, but without being self-conscious, and in the end he was almost sure: he felt he'd always known Aidi— now that's what you call a feeling, boys.

They said good-bye in an ultrachoreographed sunset, under the two towers. Finally, while he was fumbling to free his bike from its chain, Aidi walked back to him, kissed him on the cheek and ran away without turning around. Well, it's easy to understand: at that moment Alex experienced the sphincter-fibrillating sensation that something infinite had begun, something worth going to the corner bar alone to raise a toast for, knocked senseless by a barrage of joyful bombardment balls, even though with all this endlessness our young rocker's thoughts

15

weren't particularly crazy or heavy or . . . at least not for the first week.

Okay. Not even two days from that sensation ours truly—he'd already read all of cummings, obviously—was talking on the phone about her with old Helios Nardini. Alex put it out from the get-go that he was confused about the fact that in five months she'd be gone. If he got too involved—and this already seemed to be the case—the separation would hurt. Well, you know how things are between friends, especially since Alex never seemed like the type to get involved. In fact, he was always the first to start razzing someone. Anyhow, Nardini threw out the classic: "You gotta see how the Rule works. Okay? Y'know what I'm sayin'? Three days for some tongue, three weeks for a hand job, and three months for the cunt. Sorry, but that's the Rule . . . " But our old boy took it to heart right away: "Listen," he answered back to the cynic, "this is something I care about. I don't appreciate the jokes."

So this was the news.

Naturally, Nardini didn't lose a nanosecond in blabbing it to Depression Tony and all the other catholic punk amigos, dissing the poor jerk from Bologna to Switzerland. But such slimeball razzing doesn't concern us here. What counts is that old Alex really took a shot. I won't push things by saying he was—my God—*in love,* but he certainly was a bit overwhelmed, shit.

He wrote his first letter to her in those days. It was an afternoon thing, five or six pages packed with late-adolescent hopes and emotions. For the first time our rocker let himself go, discovered himself. Okay, he understood from the get-go that

16

with Aidi it wasn't like with all the other half-assed chicks from school with their "Alex I wanted to tell you I feel something for you but I don't really know what," and him, zip! ready to drop his pants to suggest an answer. All in all, Alex didn't give the slightest shit about what the girls thought or didn't think. And beyond the social convention of not yawning in someone's face when they're talking, he'd always kept the indifference index up around the fourth exponential power when dealing with the kabbalistic projections, aspirations and paranoid fears of his— my God—*partners.*

Whereas now . . . I mean he used to be *the coldest* of them all, then from one day to the next we find him a poet and de- serter from the nihilistic afternoons chilling out barefoot on Nardini's carpet and bitching about this that and the other thing with Urban Dance Squad and Rollins Band cranking and cranking harder than a Friday night traffic circle?

You got it.

As for the rest, the days passed by even in the grim and suffo- cating Liceo Caimani, and the useless hours flew between Hobbesian materialism and Mannerist critique. The teachers threatened punishment, but the preannounced showdown be- tween them and the class slackers never came. In a state of dis- belief, our old boy didn't bother to open a single book. He sat in the last row reading a collection of *Frigidaire* comics which old Hoge and that electric skull of his had lent him—comic strips and early '80s rock—the same ones Alex used to take from his uncle Sandro's shelves at his grandmother's and flip through them, oblivious of everything and immersed in the frozen age of five, lying on his back with his belly in the air while Uncle Sandro talked out loud about his medical problems.

The smell of '77, student riots, punk, the smell of tire irons under the coat. Many things started from there, from *Frigidaire,* even if Alex didn't manage to grasp all the implications. Meanwhile, with Aidi, there were hellos, smiles, little notes hidden in books and daily letters. Those were days of typing paper decorated with a sun, or a meadow, or the five-petal flower Aidi signed all her messages with. All drawn with colored pencils. She got sheets from a computer with the words printed densely, a little lighthearted, a little sad, in New York 10 point; and old Alex imagined her sitting at the table of a room he'd never seen while reading: "If you want a friend, tame me . . ."

"What do I need to do?" the little prince asked.

"You need to be very patient," the fox replied. "In the beginning you'll sit a little far from me, like this, in the grass. I'll look at you from the corner of my eye, and you won't say anything. Words are sources of misunderstanding. But day after day you'll be able to come and sit a little closer . . ."

The next day, the little prince returned.

"It would have been better to come back at the same time," the fox said. "If, for example, you arrive at four in the afternoon, I'll start being happy from three. The more time passes, the happier I'll be. When by four, I get restless and worried, I'll discover the price of happiness."

And she and Alex were *totally happy,* even through the thousand mindfucks of such a situation, even if the old boy felt a little anxious when he thought that theirs was just the story of seventeen-year-olds with a time bomb set for her departure to America.

Meanwhile, they heard from each other all the time, and when they saw each other they were happier and stronger. Each time they wanted to see each other, they'd meet downtown, wander between the bar lights, the stores, the movie theaters, talking about the little prince and how to free themselves from the conditioning of everyday life.

(One time he got there before she did and barely saw her heading his way, helmet in her hands, wearing a colored scarf. He barely recognized her from a distance, in the crowd, and he ran toward her singing without opening his mouth: they hugged, laughed, kissed each other on cold cheeks.)

They were crazy and they lived their strange dream and told each other everything and talked and laughed and walked and talked about all they'd ever seen, just like in a long dream. And then, and then

and then, one ugly day, the words between them became sources of misunderstanding. Indeed, *the* source of *a* misunderstanding, just one, but the saddest thing Alex had ever experienced

a frigid Saturday night in piazza Maggiore, Alex asked her to be his steady girl. It was the most obvious thing at that point, no?

Only.

Only she squeezed his hand tight and said she had to think about it, but she had a sad shadow in her eyes.

He came back home and felt suffocated—a feeling he couldn't quite focus in on, that he and Aidi would lose touch.

And all the following Sunday, Alex tough, Alex pissed off, Alex who couldn't give a shit, lay beat on his bed rereading *Jonathan,* my God, *Livingston Seagull,* which who else but Aidi had lent him.

Alex useless and sad as nonalcoholic beer.

From the magnetic archive of Mr. Alex D. This Sunday is the ugliest day of my life. As usual, Saturday night I go to bed late, or drink too much, and the day after is shitty because I feel sick. Anyway, Sunday is the worst day of the week. Don't even mention it. Even Leopardi and Vasco said so. All right, Vasco didn't like Mondays either, but whatever. Okay, I feel terrible, but not like I usually do . . . Aidi comes to mind and says it's better for us both if we don't see each other anymore, and I don't manage to respond—mouth wide open, heart about to go ballistic, and I can't say a word.

There, all I know is I'd miss a lot of things about her . . . sincerity . . . imagination . . . and on top of that I'm sure I've ruined a secret game, walked on crystal glasses with the grace of an elephant underwater. But the fact is I swear I don't know where I went wrong. I hurt her and I don't see how. Or maybe I hugged her too tight and now she's gotta protect herself . . .

Listening to "Love Song" by Tesla and thinking about Aidi when the song says: "Love will find the way." I feel a sort of hole in my chest, and it dawns

on me that my feelings—about *everything*—are useless,
lost, tears in the rain. Aidi will never understand
what I feel because she's holed up in her little fort.
"I'm afraid our relationship would be too exclusive,
and I care about you a lot but I'm just afraid of
giving." She could at least tell me. Because she's
got another past, another alphabet, other rimes make
her smile. We're irreconcilably different, and it's
beautiful to meet different people, but maybe it's
impossible to understand them deep down. Like that
incredible Cure song where she's all beautiful and
the poor guy looks at her and admires her and she
gets offended and Robert Smith says: "That's why I
hate you."

Anyway, he tried to find Martino around midafternoon. It was enough for Martino to hear Alex's voice saying, "Hi," to understand that our old boy was seriously bummed. They exchanged two words and decided to get together next Saturday as per the youthful formula Get Shitfaced and Crash at My Place.

Martino was two years older than Alex. He'd failed his third year in Liceo and was sort of the school's druggie idol. They started hanging out together a short while ago with a tacit pact between them: he wouldn't introduce Alex to any of his techno-house friends, and Alex wouldn't introduce him to the Fender world of parochial punk.

Then, the new week dripped by, half-assed and sad. Old Alex tried not to think of Aidi. She, on the other hand, didn't call. So our old boy tried to reduce the whole matter to one of those affairs that finish before they even start, because maybe she says, Uh, I think this thing would be too much of a commitment. Uh, let's just stay friends.

Yeah right. Let's just stay friends . . .

Once in a while they'd see each other in school for a second, during the break. Adelaide was always with her pollyanna companions, the ones in their superexpensive plush sweaters and Missoni jeans that showed—good God—two or three inches of sheer stocking. She said hi quickly, and then there was that instant where in the movie you don't know whether the two protagonists will stop and talk, that moment where he seems about to ask her, "How's it going?" but Aidi always goes away, dragged off against the flow of all the walking lobotomies that crisscrossed the hall. And him, having to wait another twenty-four hours to see her again, for just a second, and in such a situation. But Alex tough, Alex cool, would never have made the first move, so he slipped into that skewed J. Frusciante expression, like the one in the *Blood Sugar Sex Magik* booklet, and split the scene. He went to talk soccer, guitars and bitches with one of the young hounds.

Still.

Still he couldn't understand. How could she dodge him like that? How could she conform with all the other girls, their attitudes and shitty little tricks. How could she have those scrap heaps of global adolescence as friends?

Because she was different, that was as plain as the nose on your face. She seemed out of place pulling such bullshit, the little chick that tries to avoid a guy that's coming on too strong, and so on.

* * *

(Shut into the adolescent bitterness of those days, he discovered a Vasco album lost under the bed: "Crazy Sunday," "There's Only Us," "Mashed Liver" and "I Love You—You Just Don't Know.")

From the magnetic archive of Mr. Alex D. She watches me a second too long, passing beside me with her kotex friends. You can see for miles she can see I'm sad. But she won't even come and tell me. Low point.

Martino seemed straight out of a European Community–funded documentary about today's youth. In fact, he was the teenager every director dreams of: a better than decent body, clothes conscious—Fred Perry, Polo, designer sweaters, Doc Martens shoes—he had a street gang vocabulary and a blue pseudo-proletarian Vespa. But he was full of money. His parents had been divorced for ages. His mother was now with some right-wing dickhead.

The right-wing dickhead showered him with precious jazz on vinyl to placate his own guilt complex. Martino gave them to Alex in the name of bebop.

(They're not that different, jazz and punk. If you think about it, there's the same marginalization, the same rage inside. And there's smack behind both of them.)

Nothing was ever said about Martino's real father, and Martino didn't like to talk about his family. Anyway, he and Alex had become friends one night in January, in a pub on via del Pratello. It looked like Martino was Valentina's new boyfriend. She was one of the few girls Alex knew who'd been kicked out of the Evervirgin Sorority. He and Martino kicked up a conversation about music around the big Oktoberfest table. Both liked ska, Madness, the Specials, Sham 69. Both went to England in the summer. Alex was sent to a cardboard version made for Milanese tourists so he could learn phrasal verbs; while Martino mixed with mysterious locals, drinking and puking, breaking chairs and drinking and.

That night, after a couple of Guinnesses and countless De Niro smiles directed at one of Valentina's pollyanna friends, who Alex didn't even like and who would've gone on for two months about how he was after her but didn't have the guts to say it, Alex left to go to the toilet. Martino followed him, leaving the girls at the mercy of Nardini and his Eurail adventures, which all of Bologna knew by heart.

Alex liked to get up and leave the group because everyone knows that the minute you get up the girls start talking about you. And he liked that. Maybe they don't say the same things they whisper to your face, maybe they take you apart, bad-mouth you. But they make you the center of attention, right? Sure enough. In any case it's not that Alex felt particularly worthy of attention at that moment. The girls would probably be busy talking about Martino, who was out with them for the first time as Valentina's new guy and therefore in the spotlight.

Alex liked Martino's way of speaking and acting—detached. As for the rest, Martino didn't read, didn't write, had gotten together with one of his old flirts, didn't play music or sports, and was the classic cool dude who knew everyone and his mother. Alex should've hated a guy like that. Instead, he wanted to be his friend right off the bat.

(He hated looking at himself in the mirror. Especially Saturday night: glassy eyes, rosy cheeks, messy hair. He always cut it short, like Flea, the Chili Peppers' bass player—even if it didn't suit him. He cut it that way with an electric razor he'd bought in England, even though the Chancellor and the Matron tried any way they could to prevent him. Still it was cool. In front of the bathroom mirror. Dinnertime by now. Fluorescent light and bzzz-zzz-zzz. Instant suede-head. Anarchy rules. Kinda like in the dressing room before a concert.)

Martino approached the mirror over the sink and passed the back of his hand under his throat, sticking his chin out like he was checking his facial growth. The only false move Alex could've held against him. As for the rest, old Martino was impeccable.

He made his way to the back of the bathroom, brushing against the urinal as he walked, and planted himself under a frosty window that opened out on a lightless courtyard, letting the frozen air inside. Then he broke out the Rizla papers, the Drum, the dope and proceeded to roll up.

"Got a bus ticket?" Martino asked Alex.

"I ride a bike," he replied. "No ticket. Sorry."

Martino shrugged his shoulders. "No biggie. We'll make it filterless."

Alex didn't say anything. Maybe he felt a little nervous, seeing as how he whipped out a Magic Marker pilfered from the stationery store by the school and threw himself into a particularly exacting task—an inscription of "Clash City Rockers" on the toilet seat. An inscription (let it be said in understated terms) that wasn't as demented as "Go Virtus" or "Baggio you're beautiful" or the phone number of some chick who's supposed to give serious blow jobs free of charge . . .

As if they *really* existed, chicks that give blow jobs for free. No way. They all want either money or social status. Well, not *all*. Some want *both*.

All that aside, Martino was as concentrated as a bomb defuser. He finished rolling, and the spliff had an exultant, complete quality to it. It was fucking perfect. Not too conical, not too skinny, a little longer than a normal cigarette. From innumerable angles it looked like some sort of magic Moroccan cigar.

Alex continued his toilet script with the earnestness of a devotee. "Shit," he thought, "fine fucking figure." And when Martino fished his Zippo from his pocket, Alex wanted to say, well—without sounding like Pinocchio's Geppetto—that uh, he felt . . . well, you know . . . sort of uneasy, and like . . . as far as he was concerned, to smoke . . . or not to smoke . . . Well, he'd rather not smoke. There. Brrr!

And it's not like Alex was worried about seeming uncool. Let's try to see it from his point of view. Alex was pretty straight, and it wasn't right for him to smoke with a stranger, just as it didn't seem right, brrr! to have Sex with a girl to Just Do It. (Later, fortunately, one grows up, and certain convictions disappear down the shithole to the sound of sweet Muzak.)

"Sorry, Chief, I'm not into it." The voice came out fine, I mean he didn't come across like some sort of geek. At that point Martino could've said: "What, are you stupid or something? This ain't dirt weed! . . ." Instead, nothing. He took a particularly inspired hit and whispered: "No problem, buddy." Meanwhile the smell of pot danced all around. As for me, a person who's up on the facts, I'd just like to add this: Martino didn't think Alex was a geek. Likewise, Alex didn't consider him among the ranks of the half-assed-wannabe-burnout-posers.

Indeed, a few weeks later—it might be interesting to note—Martino admitted in person that he came to respect Alex on just that occasion, because our old boy didn't feel he had to smoke if he didn't want to. You see, that's how Martino was: he could throw a shit fit if someone looked at him the wrong way, and he was definitely the kind of guy who liked to scrap, or instigate a brawl on Saturday night between the Bologna boys and the out-of-towners in the disco, or between students and locals on a field trip, and so on. But he would do *anything,* non-violent and kind, for a friend.

Martino felt at ease in any situation, even when someone else would've fucked off. He went around with a switchblade in the pocket of his bomber. He didn't have to answer to anybody. I mean, if he came home with a broken hand or all slashed up, no one would give him the third degree.

Alex also loved to drink and slam and mosh and generally rave it up as much as anyone. But he could never afford to take a chair across his back or a bottle in the face. Anyway, he tended to cruise through calmer circles. So it goes without saying

That Saturday afternoon, before getting the night of serious drinking under way, he walked into Martino's house for the first time all sweaty and uneasy. Fortunately there was no one in a penguin suit or apron furrowing the house's superexpensive halls. The decor looked frighteningly similar to the house of the woman whom the ultravivacious protagonist of *A Clockwork Orange* bludgeoned to death with the help of your standard ceramic cock: Old Paintings, Hunting Rifles, Tapestries, the Komplete Kollection of Blue Plates from Denmark . . .

Martino's room was exactly the way Alex had imagined it though: the classic lair of someone who does his own thing and gets whatever he wants from the rest of the inhabitants. I mean people who manage to stay around him without *suffocating* him.

Anyway, it was like a real pad, though the room was anything but small. Only it was *full*. Chockablock full like in that goddam Timberland ad: posters everywhere, clothes everywhere, Peruvian blankets all over the place, photos all over the place.

Old Alex could have stayed in there for hours just to know the names of the guys camped out on the cork panel over the bed; or to read the titles on the spines of the CD's and videos. For the books, however, a nanosecond would have been enough: thrown in to hold up the collection of *Max* and *Ciak* magazines.

Lying inert in their glacial solitude, there was a *Brothers Karamazov,* a collection of Hemingway stories, a couple of books on Pink Floyd and a brand-new English dictionary.

The collection of videos was mind-blowing though: everything by Woody Allen, everything by Scorsese, all of Coppola and Kubrick, all the latest Verhoeven, everything by Malle, Kurosawa, the legendary Aki Kaurismaki, Oliver Stone, *Giant, Rebel without a Cause, East of Eden,* five or six films with Brando, and even some things with actors which our generation has rarely heard mentioned: Jean Gabin, Louis De Funes, Peter Sellers. If you want to stretch it a little, it would've already been something if old Alex had seen less than half of all that stuff. And then Fellini, Risi senior, Ferreri. Nan-ni Mo-ret-ti! France-scAr-chi-bu-gi!

Cool. Apart from that, Martino welcomed him in a swank checkered night robe thrown over a pair of pajamas made of some material he couldn't focus in on precisely since he was used to the normal denim of jeans and the grungy Pakistani cotton of concert T-shirts with rock stars on them: play it loud, wear it proud.

From the magnetic archive of Mr. Alex D. Sincerely, I'm pretty impressed by Martino . . . He must really be at peace with himself. He must've reached a helluva balance inside himself to walk around in a nightshirt all combed and shaved, wallowing in the scent of aftershave and mint toothpaste. Someone like that can only be happy. I'm sure.

A real character, Martino. He gave certain as-
pects of life a miss in order to follow the ones he
liked. Still, the fact that he gave up his studies
and sports to dedicate himself full-time to girls,
movies and trips abroad irks me a little.

But I have to know more. Understand better.

Martino is full of interesting attitudes. Only
it's giving me a whole bunch of complexes. I feel
like a clueless loser compared to him. I mean he
sometimes makes me feel that way. Like he does everything he can to make me feel at ease, but shit, I'll
never be like him. I mean like he goes to the beauty
salon for his blackheads, good god · · ·

All right. I swear I'll buy me a pair of nice
pajamas and velvet slippers too.

(In those days, old Alex's consciousness could feel something
elbowing its way inside: the certainty that in order to appear so
utterly well-off, even when alone—and this without anyone
being there to judge—he must've developed a pretty high opin-
ion of himself. Whereas Alex was always in bed with his boxer
shorts and walked around the house in sweatpants and a T-shirt,
or a sweatshirt when it was cold, with those threadbare slippers.
So what the hell was this all about? I mean on an introspective
level.)

The panel of photos extended over the length of the bed and was
more than three feet high. Not much room for guitar heroes

or stadium idols in that series. For the most part they were of Martino playing the lion: Martino infant, in the arms of maybe his mother; Martino with a bib eating what's left of the ice cream he smeared all over his face; Martino smiling in the arms of maybe his father. Next was a series on the masquerade theme with Martino dressed up as the favorite characters of the under-ten crowd of that time: Martino-Zorro, Martino-Sandokan, Martino-Goldrake et cetera, up to a sort of Martino-samurai armed with a conspicuous plastic sword and plumed combat helmet. Then, in the next to last series, Martino in the arms of his mother's friends. Veteran '68ers now rich editors, liberal lawyers and untenured professors. All people that didn't live to show off, with monumental sideburns, big flower-power shirts and some of the most outlandish mustaches and bell-bottoms of the period. Then finally: Martino in the arms of his father's ex–college buddies, poses exhibiting the traits of a sports champion, teeth in order, loads of money and so on. Going through these photos one by one, old Alex wasn't surprised that Martino's parents wound up separating. On top of that: he could imagine them, the poison darts from her Trotskyite friends aimed at his jock friends and vice versa. Now, in any case, Martino's mother kept Marx's *Das Kapital* and the Bolivian diaries of Commandante Che lined up neatly in the library of the villa in the hills where she lived with her son, supported by her ex-husband, perfectly at ease in the role of a lady in Clarks shoes who makes use of her Proletariat Past only to give her new free-entrepreneurial-mason-rot-aryan friends a few shudders.

In the last photo of the series, there was Martino with a couple of girls Alex had caught a glimpse of in the hallways at school. They seemed happy.

"Who knows who took the photos?" old Alex asked himself.

(If you really feel good with a girl, it must be hard to find someone who'll take a picture of you without ruining everything by saying you're not smiling enough. You've got to be real careful with someone who's happy.)

What made old Alex really cave in on himself was the idea that Martino had presumably found happiness without particularly committing himself to any activity, without too much thought and hardly any inhuman emotional trips, just like that, simply. There in that Timberland ad of a crib, a doubt began to gnaw at him: maybe inner balance, nirvana, wasn't really a condition to attain—in the sense of *chasing* it—the way the Chancellor, the Matron, and the semi-Prussian propaganda of Liceo Caimani insisted.

From the magnetic archive of Mr. Alex D. In the end, inner balance isn't something you can look for. Maybe we have it already, and the more we get stirred up or move or whatever, the further away it gets. The fact is just talking about inner balance makes me feel like a dipshit. It seems like one of those terms used in group therapy sessions or in battered women's shelters.

Okay. Everything tells me to be strong, sure about
my goals, able to move ahead in Life, but if you feel
the moment to change gears a little has come, or even
just to stop and think *seriously* on your own? I mean
just take an A in Latin for example; good grades have
gone from being simple tools to ends in and of themselves . . . Anyway, as much as I know I gotta study
to get a diploma, which will get me a good job, which
in turn will get me enough money to get some friggin
serenity—all massacred and war-wounded by the incredible efforts it took to get it. It's like this
martyr's serenity is one of the ends in and of themselves. That's how the logic works. It doesn't take
a genius. So why do I have to sacrifice those moments of serenity that come to me *spontaneously* on
the street? Why should I throw them down into a well
if they're part of the desired end? If one afternoon
I can go and jam a little or go out with a girl I
like, why the hell should I stay home and transcribe
my Latin homework straight from the translation, or
pretend to read some Philosophy? The reality is that
I find myself obliged to sacrifice the happy seventeen-year-old me of this afternoon for an eventual
bald, overweight, content fifty-year-old me who opens
the garage door by remote control, has a nice car
inside, a wife who probably cheats on him with the
accountant and two twin kids with bowl-cut hairdos
that look like Hitler Youth. All inside the garage,
I bet. Let's say more or less *around*. Like *surrounded*.

35

So the question is: can a horror show of such proportions be worth more than this afternoon's sun and
ice cream? More than whatever girl? More than Valentina
arriving ten minutes late for a date with a smile on
her face and a blue T-shirt with those two wondrous
gifts from God inside?

I mean the photos of Martino gave me a *real*
insight into the whole sham: it's enough to just stay
put and take whatever comes your way, shit · · ·

Okay, so Martino practically lives the life of
a young country gentleman, holed up on his estate
with barber appointments marked on his calendar,
hardly any commitments and plenty of privileges. In
theory we should hate each other, seeing how yours
truly comes from the most middle-class family there
is—a sort of mini-war machine that's molded me into
the Work Hard to Reach Your Objectives and don't
risk becoming an Adult Full of Regrets strategy.
Okay. My folks'll be happy. I'm so determined and
such a go-getter war machine myself that I *already*
have regrets.

I don't know, but at Martino's house, while I
was looking at those damn photos, I had the horrible
sensation of killing all those happy boys, one by
one, day after day · · · Because maybe I could've been
that happy too. All right, so I'm not filthy rich
like Martino. But that's not *essential* for being happy.
I mean you can live well even without a lot of money.

But maybe things are even *worse*. Why didn't I go
after what I wanted? It's like I give myself an abor-
tion every day, like I can't let that boy be born for
fear of tripping over him, for fear of him upsetting
my life. This way I've always allowed myself little
bits of styrofoam happiness: going to the park, staying
home all afternoon, watching MTV instead of studying, cutting class, pigging out, jerking myself off
with particular devotion . . .

You could see for miles that Martino went out of his way not to
make Alex feel uptight about being used to more hard-core
Saturday nights—driving to the beach at Riccione, for starters,
surrounded by sundry slutty seventeen-year-old girls—than the
8:10 show at the Rainbow cinema, with Depression Tony to his
right and Helios Nardini to his left, and Abatantuono and
Claudio Bisio as soldiers in Greece on the screen.

So in order not to make him feel uptight about their dif-
ferences on this Saturday night where Alex was to follow the
formula Get Shitfaced and Crash at My Place, Martino went to
one of the usual café-bars on via del Pratello with Alex to con-
sume multiple brewskies; and then the flawless one pulled a
C-note out of his wallet when the check came.

They finished by telling each other the most picturesque
episodes of their respective lives, and Martino was simply un-
beatable in the bar. They talked and laughed and talked while
the blood alcohol level rose with inexorable calm; then they went
outside to raise some hell in the Bologna night, racing from San

Domenico to the Cavour gallery, ringing doorbells—miss! miss! please, open up, my friend's hurt he's had an accident!—pissing against the walls and garbage cans and other silly undertakings that make you so giddy you can tell yourself it's finished with Aidi and everything'll still be totally cool.

By the time they parked themselves in piazza Minghetti old Alex was already trashed. Cotton hood over his head, sitting with his arms crossed and good night. Anyway, there were no time limits this night, no third degrees like young man what have you been drinking, how much did you spend, you smell like smoke . . .

He had no idea what time it was, and Martino woke him up with a few head butts. Alex felt his eyes all bleary, and the flawless one wanted to drag him down to strada Maggiore to see if the little place was open that he knew served a killer green beer at just about all hours.

But first they wrestled on the ground.

After the wrestling match Martino jumped on Alex's belly and immobilized his wrists, numb to the knees Alex was pounding into his back. It took some time after they'd gotten up to figure out—between a few resolute sniffs and reciprocally unmentioned suspicions—that they'd been rolling around in a carpet of dog shit.

(It was already light, so they took the road home.)

Martino drove the scooter and old Alex was perched behind him with his throat all dry. While he was adjusting the Blues Brothers glasses on his nose, the frozen wind gave him a few slaps under his eyes, which were embroidered with the implacable shreds of a concentrically disintegrating and unrepeatable instant-karma: the coarse fabric of his gray German army surplus jacket, worries about the physics test on Monday he still hadn't studied for (which was all right since it was multiple choice and he could easily copy), Martino's shaved nape an inch away from his boxer's nose, the dial of his watch with scratched glass: the blue hands indicated a time which Alex estimated between five thirty and quarter to six in the morning. More like quarter to six though. Never could understand a thing with that shitty watch.

He could've been someone else, in another place. Instead he was there, perched behind Martino riding full throttle up and down the hilly streets in a cold, pale morning with a cyberpunk headache from all the yakkety-yakking and nonsense and anguish and beer they'd indulged in on that strange two-dog juvenile night.

(The two of them were cruising on the scooter, and Aidi lived right there, behind the TV antenna. Further down, at the base of the hill, there was a cluster of houses wrapped in fog.)

For a split second old Alex thought about asking Martino to take him there so he could wake her up, sit beside her bed and talk to her. Then it dawned on him that Martino would've really done it, take him there that is, and so he figured it was better not to say anything and just keep drying his eyes which were tearing from the cold behind his glasses.

It was about six, and old Alex felt his throat burning and his lips all chapped when Martino hit the brakes, skidding hard in front of the gate to his house; and at twelve sharp of that same Sunday it was show time again, for Alex—cadaverous youth on the day of our Lord—had to take part in the mass at St. Joseph's church from an out of range position in the back.

His brother was up front somewhere with the boyscouts.

Even Alex had been a boyscout way back when: cub, explorer, novice, and finally a rover. He detested the happy family rhetoric and the moronic practical jokes, though that was the best group he'd ever hung out with. In the end he left, understandably, but he continued to see the others, his sublime, alcoholic and ever-rebel friends . . .

"Today Christ is wounded. Today Christ is marginalized. Today Christ is outlawed. Today, brothers and sisters, Jesus Christ begs on the streets." The missionary friar went into one of his most successful and rhetorical pauses. He attracted still more attention to himself, and a second later, after having lowered his gaze, almost as if to ask forgiveness in advance for some blunder he couldn't keep from making, he put his hands on the lectern and squeezed like he was about to pull it up from the roots, then quickly raised his eyes. Alex couldn't keep from making a small gesture of dismay; the monk's gaze had something fiery about it, the veins in his temples and neck became swollen like the result of some mutation. In a curious but firm way, the priest looked like Lou Ferrigno as the Incredible Hulk, and the Hulk was announcing to his flock that Christ had actually been condemned and suffered in prison.

Nothing more probable, Alex thought to himself, even if he couldn't stop hoping for some sort of miraculous amnesty that would've allowed old Jesus to come in the flesh, ASAP, right there in St. Joe Schmo Husband of Virgin Mary Church to give all those fifty-year-old farts in the choir—crying in ecstasy, tinkling their jewelry and smearing their makeup—a good ass kicking. Sure, Father Ferrigno's missionary sermon must've moved them to the core, the assholes—forced to finally open their eyes, helped to understand the nameless hypocrisy which *we* are capable of . . .

(And we're truly Christians, in a manner of speaking. Though faith is something else.)

. . . The missionary monk is right to say that faith has lived side by side with the poor, the derelict, the marginal, all those folks who fortunately don't live on via Saragozza. Anyway, we do need more charity. Deep down though, you can realize and spread the Christian message even in the richest societies. As a matter of fact, it's probably easier here. I can talk about it at the shitty rot-aryan meetings on Friday night, and we can organize a fund-raiser for Yugoslavia or Af-frica. Even in Af-frica they suffer, those poor children . . . Yes, yes, a nice little donation is all it takes. And then we'll buy a new Fiat for Piergiangi, who's twenty-four by now and can't drive that old VW Rabbit all his life, no? The Rabbit we'll pass on to Maria Stuarda Betty, who's already eighteen! . . .

Alex *tried* to believe in God, but the biggest problem was all the butt-head hypocrites he met in church. This included all the catechism youngsters who livened up the Mass with guitars, and the choir of virgins in blouses and skirts down to their ankles. It seemed to him a public relations ploy, understand? It's become necessary because of the collapse of the Church, the fact that fewer and fewer young people want to go to Mass. A helluva move, and not even covert at that, to enlarge the target and get all the twelve-year-olds with braces in their mouths to become just like them, organizing benefit fishing trips, playing the guitar, going to vocational camps and singing Mount Zion duets and going for pizza with the confirmation group and getting a significant other and getting married and making love and putting away rainy day money and becoming poor happy assholes.

Alex suspected that in reality the priest and the other monks hated the catechism youth who livened up the masses with their guitars and their Evervirgin-in-blouse-and-skirt-down-to-the-ankles choir. But the fact is that the priest and monks *needed* them now. "Watch out assholes," Alex thought, "because in the times of the Latin rite y'all with braces in your mouths would've lined yourselves up against the wall and ready-aim-fire and that's that."

Two *Never Mind the Bollocks* later it was Monday morning again, and he hath yet to study his physics.

He got to school twenty minutes early with a lump in his throat—a feeling of remorse quite similar to the one he used to get as a kid after having pilfered the tasty cakes from the Matron's dispenser.

In two late-adolescent words, there was a physics test and old Alex ain't studied a *muddah-funkin thing*. Late-adolescent moral: the young schmuck who reads *Frigidaire* and music-that's-not-music-but-noise magazines during physics class, finds himself with six chapters to cram, and instead of covering his ass hangs out with bad influences on the eve of the test, engaging in acts of petty hooliganism in the company of a friend he'd be better off without.

That's cool though. Now he'd get his just *punishment,* and all that other fucked up stuff that goes with Catholicism.

His drawers were already crawling up his crotch, so Alex tried to assess the situation from on high, like a general in difficulty standing over a map, planning a diversionary maneuver. Oscar was home for three days with a self-induced flu so he could study Greek, which meant he couldn't copy off Oscar; the Baron knew even less than Alex, so that was a no-go as well; the other possibilities were all too far away from his position, ergo . . .

He thought about it all Sunday night, when the guilt trips were keeping him from falling asleep. He'd passed the first test by the skin of his teeth, and it would've been a crime to screw it up with the thermodynamic debacle that was waiting for him. He'd already had seven absences, so there were still two strategic cuts available before they checked up on him . . .

As he was assessing the diversionary maneuver on the map from on high, old Alex caught sight of the Social-Democrat from his class, the one who wears Docksides and old fogy shirts. They exchanged pats on the back. "Hey dude," Alex said. "How about cutting class?"

"Serious? Excellent!" The Social-Democrat gave it a thought, but then the asshole didn't follow through. In fact he was already covering his tracks: "Too bad I got Latin though," he said all trembling and flushed in the face. "But next time we'll all get together before and do a megacut, deal?"

(Yeah right. Megacut my ass.)

Anyhow, the asshole's eyes were shining, and maybe the temptation to get rid of that Jollinvicta backpack and unlock his bike had him for a nanosecond, but then his eyes turned opaque again and he offered the world its gazillionth half-assed performance: "Like I'll see ya then. I guess you'll be there when we get out?"

Dickhead.

"Go fuck yourself," old Alex muttered under his breath, "up the wazoo." Then he threw in a gosh-darned "Maybe" all useless and sad as nonalcoholic beer.

The trouble with the Social-Democrat was that he never wanted to disappoint anyone. The poor schmuck went out of his way to show he liked everything and got along with everyone, but without letting anyone know what he did to make others happy and what he did because he really wanted to.

There are those who like guys like this.

Then, when the usual janitors opened the doors, and all the walking lobotomies of Liceo Caimani crowded up to the entrance, our rocker was pierced by a single thought: "Get out of this absurd tussle, ASAP"

Old Alex was sitting on the portico railing, beyond range of the river of Jollinvictas and Mandarina Ducks seething impetuously. All the first-year students entered en masse, with maybe fifteen minutes to go before the bell. They'd already been there for a while, like fired up groupies at a concert waiting for the gates to open. Alex used to do this too, back in Middle School, and wouldn't even hang out for a bull session or stop for a chat. During recess he'd stay in class playing soccer or writing in his—my God—diary. And forget about loitering in the halls.

And yet those were the appointments not to be missed. But he only understood that at the end: that the only place where it wasn't important to be was at the entrance. Unless he didn't have anyone to cut class with, as was the case now. Anyhow he could hardly believe it, because he was sure he knew everyone in school, at least by sight—but actually it was always the same twenty or thirty celebrities making the rounds. Whereas this underworld, this horde of punctual dorks, he couldn't remember ever seeing them.

"This must be the first time all year I got here early," he said to himself, puzzled, eyes wide open staring at all the pimple-faced monsters with all those ridiculous haircuts, braces and twittering sweat jackets from Middle School. They moved in groups like crazy adolescent monsters. In crews. In clubs.

Who knows how many houses, who knows how many families, more or less middle class, were behind those monsters; and who knows how many closets full of clothes, how many mothers who said Robertamaria don't ever do this because you're *very* cute and it's the boys who don't know what they want . . .

Old Alex tried to annihilate all the bodies and set fire to their underwear and that's that. He could've used some of Clark Kent's X-ray vision, sure, but the idea was fascinating, admit it: all the hundreds of panties, and slips and bras of all shapes and sizes in motion. Worthy of Stephen King in a way.

Then Alex caught sight of the first familiar faces. Bungani with the camouflage jacket stuffed with illicit substances; Tito Scarpa on crutches; old Cico dressed like a leftist radical, veteran of the Island squatters' community; Mazza with his helmet in his hand; De Luca with De Luca's new girlfriend. And then his class, framed amidst the heap: an opaque zone of unfriendly, unintelligent, asexual types, plus a patrol of his real and depressive friends hanging out with a couple of public interest babes. Finally, there was Rinaldi, old Hoge's friend, unshakable with his denim jacket, acne and crew cut. He was one of the nicest guys. A guy who never ever went anywhere. A bunch of times Alex wondered how this guy could feel so good about himself, so spontaneous, without any prejudices in that school full of festering assholes. He probably didn't *really* feel good about himself, was the conclusion Alex came to.

Hoge told him that Rinaldi always wound up talking about Gross Sex, that he was one of these smiling happy maniacs, and every time one of their female friends would get up to go to the bathroom or throw something in the trash Rinaldi would whisper: "She's got a couple of nice pears growing there, no?" and from there he'd take off into fantasies that got way out of hand. In fact old Hoge's electric head couldn't take sitting on the bench with the guy anymore because his unmentionable fantasies got him too worked up.

The rest of the time, when there were no chicks around that had to get up and go to the bathroom or throw something away or whatever, Rinaldi read big English books like *The History of Apple Computers,* and you could say he was a pillar of the bathroom crew.

Every teacher has his own shtick. Old Alex & Co. knew the whole routine by heart: there was the one who asked questions first, then explained; the one who sometimes asked questions and sometimes explained; and then there was the Italian teacher who lectured on Bembo and Castiglione and a few other stiffs until the end of November, surrounded by a tomblike indifference.

During the questions it was no problem. You could stay outside and come in without losing much. But if you turned around in class scratching your balls, snorting out of your nose or scuffing your feet on the floor during a fiery lecture on Hesiod

47

or some unQEDable equation or the rings of Saturn, you could bet the teacher would take it personally. In the course of such a gripping lesson it's advisable to catapult yourself into it halfway through—a simple desperate expression of a monosyllabic nature to make it seem like you got lost helps things—then plunge headlong into the fray, take notes furiously as if catching up, zoom in on the blackboard with steely determination and raise your hand at the appropriate moment to ask a pretentious yet plausible question. If you follow the procedure correctly, the teacher will have retained a vaguely positive impression of you on a subconscious level at lesson's end.

If there was any risk of getting a "come here, young man," then you just stayed out. The only teachers who went out searching for fugitives were the ones least interested of all, the teachers who didn't care about giving a good lesson, only how many empty seats there were in class. These do-nothing teachers were worse: they had a dirty conscience and tried to fuck you over every time.

So whoever split first would peer into the classes of the rest of the bathroom crew, and with a discrete sign that the teacher couldn't see would call who he had to. Old Alex liked to catch the gaze of some self-composed babe, make Johnny Rotten faces and point to the desired homeboy. After two or three twists of the face, the babe-of-choice caught on and turned in the right direction to point the door out to Hoge or Rinaldi or Depression Tony or Leo Chernobyl, and the untouchable would rise up, give the situation a good eyeball and split for the exit with his head down so the teacher couldn't see he was smiling.

They drank warm beer in the bathroom. Heineken which they'd bought at the supermarket the day before, then hid in the fridge at home. Of course it was warm again by now. But Alex thought it was great to leave class with a can hidden under his shirt and hook up with all his parochial punk friends in the hall, their heads sticking out of the johns, making a sign to hurry up before he got spotted by one of hall monitors that the principal guided by remote control.

(The john was the most beautiful place in Caimani. A place where no one came to bust your balls, where you could talk about the reviews in *Blast* magazine or virtual reality or rubbers or rock concerts at the New Church, Sant' Egidio, Santa Rita.)

During those years full of phony slobs, as Holden Caulfield would say, Alex felt more in tune with the revolutionary heads of Negu Gorriak and the Pistols' "Anarchy in the U.K." than with Xenophon's *Anabasis*.

The bathroom crew even talked politics. They considered themselves reds, radicals, anarchists. They hated the asshole Nazis that proliferated through the school, sons of sons of merchants, accountants and dentists, children of an unpenitent Italyun ignorance. And the Nazis hated them. The bathroom crew felt, with various nuances between them, part of a smiling and sincere left. They sympathized with the underground world of squatters and indie record labels. And more than anything, they hated the fat-assed Pinocchios of organized political parties.

* * *

(In the city, the party bosses had authorized the eviction of all the squatters' centers, like the Island and the Factory. They proclaimed broad-mindedly that Bologna was a place which had practically attained Socialism with a human face, then descended from their hilltop villas in Benzes to distribute phony pre- or postelectoral smiles every time the Virtus played basketball at home.)

(They were nothing but Pinocchios and VIP scumbags, as D. D. Bombay used to roar in Splatter Pink's demo. And their children, Pierdavide, Gianfrancesco, Camillamaria, stayed in class to veg out in the void, thinking about how to piss away three bills on Saturday night, flashing that shit-eating grin at the teacher talking about the Commune of Paris.)

Even this was somewhat of a class struggle for old Alex and his friends. A war between those who had to bust their asses and those who had the good fortune to be born rich or have parents deft at finding tax loopholes. And then there were all the eighteenth-birthday parties in villas with shit-for-breath rot-aryan fathers in masonic hoods all tan from tennis tournaments, no?

The oldest ones from the bathroom crew, old enough to vote, leaned toward the Communists, though. Or, like Alex, they espoused the ideas and programs of the antiprohibition Libertarians.

Whatever.

We left off where Alex saw Rinaldi, right?

"What's up, dude?" old Alex addressed him.

"Hey. What are you, *early* today?"

Old Alex shrugged his shoulders. You could see he was bummed.

"So," Rinaldi said. "What classes you got this morning?"

He smelled it right off the bat. There was no doubt.

"Two hours of *Greek*," Alex threw out at him, eyes vibrating with extraordinary hope. "History and a fucking physics test . . . Listen, what d'ya say we cut today? Cuz look, I really don't know what to do."

Alex looked straight through him, terribly direct, and old Rinaldi scratched his chin.

He was into it. He was way into it.

He just needed to be reassured a little, and old Alex was a master when it came to reassuring.

(Moments of lacerating intensity follow in which the lashes of adrenaline came in flocks from every which way.)

Then Mrs. Boriani from Chemistry passed by and Alex pulled Rinaldi into the shadow—"It's Boriani. Don't let her see you"— and Rinaldi dove into the porticoes' shadow zone, fluid as a dolphin, because one time Boriani had seen him outside of school when he was cutting, and Rinaldi didn't even realize he'd been seen. The next morning, when he went to hand in his excuse— Grave Family Reasons—the old bag came out with "Imagine that, Rinaldi, I believe I saw you yesterday. Here, in front of the school."

He's there looking like a cross between a priest accused of sexually abusing the kids in catechism class and the sad grandson. He shook his head briskly and said: "Yesterday, unfortunately, that wasn't possible. My family and I were all in Parma for my uncle's funeral."

They must've heard the story of the defunct uncle hundreds of times, but when Rinaldi said: "No, no, we were all in Parma," the laughs and snickers of approval rose up to high heaven. It wasn't so simple an idea in the end. Anyone could've thought up the idea of a relative's funeral, but the majesty of that geographic detail, with that touch of family life in *Parma*? Now that was classy. You could just see him. Old Rinaldi, as a child going to Parma with his family to visit this engineer uncle now gone.

You almost felt sorry for this nonexistent uncle.

Cool. Alex and Rinaldi split for the Artist's Bar, refuge of every cut organizer worthy of respect, and for a second Alex saw himself in the bar's mirror and liked what he saw: gray shirt buttoned up to the top, supershort hair, Schott jeans with ultraironed hems and shiny shoes with a yellow stripe visible on the rubber of his platform soles. Then, as he daydreamed about ever more radical haircuts and the West Ham United emblem he wanted to sew on either his army or his bomber jacket to shock the bourgeoisie, Aidi came to mind. She was probably about fifty yards away, outside the school, and he felt like he was in a movie and wanted to run after her, shouting like that, without a jacket, with a half-eaten sandwich and a bottle in his hand, see her from a distance all colorful as she's talking to the other girls in black and white, elbow his way through everyone in his trajectory until he was next to her and just ask her *"Why?"* and then start it all from the top again, because you could see for miles that it wasn't finished between them, and even she knew it all too well. And it was decided, shit: once back home, that afternoon, he would write her a letter that left no room for misunderstandings, and within four or five days that absurd situation would be finished.

Fifteen minutes later, old Hoge, who'd just come from the Benfe bar, showed up and wanted to gather the boys together. Every now and then another truant would come in with his books and helmet. The guys at the bar served coffee and were having a bull session with the adult clients. Rinaldi was the first to scratch the silence that had engulfed their table in the corner. The silence, and that other feeling that came over all three of them, wasn't exactly a feeling of nostalgia for the way it had been forty minutes earlier, when they were all still in their own beds, with posters and photos hanging behind their heads and the blankets crumpled up between their legs, but it made them all a little sad nonetheless, and they had to just spit it out of their minds.

"Listen," Rinaldi said, crossing his arms irrevocably. "Now we're all gonna go to my place."

"Deal," Alex said, exchanging a look of acknowledgment with Hoge. "Sure. Where do you live?"

They left their backpacks and jackets on Rinaldi's bed in the room he shared with a younger brother who was in a phase of Matchbox cars, tabletop football and sports heroes posters.

From the furnishings you could tell Rinaldi's family wasn't particularly rich—and yet they weren't particularly poor, but more or less the national average; and as such *below* that of the liceo, populated for the most part by kids of classic car collectors, landowners, et cetera. Maybe this thing about car collector fathers and all was just a particular and didn't really mean much.

Yeah, maybe, but it counted all the same.

In a society where a seventeen-year-old doesn't feel like sharing a room with someone who has cheaper luggage than his, there are a lot of particulars that count.

Old Alex liked Rinaldi and wished all his friends could be like him, open about their neighborhood roots, remembering the courtyards they ran around in as kids and the afternoons spent gathering telephone tokens left by grown-ups when the old phone booths with their yellow coin return buttons were still around. Alex leaned against the living room sofa, next to Hoge and his washed-out sweatshirt. Rinaldi was already doing stuff to break the ice and put everyone at ease. At one point he laid out a spread worthy of old Burgess—ice cold vodka and some cookies. The howls of approval reached the sky.

With a fluid and nervous hand, Alex flipped the contents of the opaque shot glass unhurriedly into his gullet. Hoge didn't hesitate to tell us the one about the Sardinian who offered to fuck the thirty-foot gorilla. And then there were the cookies, those awesome Mulino Bianco hug cookies that went with vodka like a marriage made in heaven, Christ. Hugs didn't exist when they were kids: all they had were frolls, the ones with honey or granulated sugar, and a few others that already seemed great compared to those dry tea biscuits that melted in the tea before you had a chance to pull them out.

Rinaldi threw on some Pink Floyd.

Then the conversation turned to soccer.

Sociologically sublime!

In the end, talking about soccer at Caimani was a way of differentiating yourself from the multitudes of tennis twits and tanned ski freaks that infested the air. Because soccer for the youth in Italy means splashing around in a field full of mud, tearing the skin off your knees in the courtyard, waking up early on Sunday and pedaling through the fog to go to practice with all the buddies from the Cheetah Soccer club.

Having an interest in soccer or rugby or boxing or cycling, in any given scholastic environment, was like claiming you were outside the cotton-puff world of the other spoiled seventeen-year-olds. It meant you knew how to hang out in bars, talk to the barber and get home at night on your own when the scooter breaks down and you don't have any money for a taxi. In two late-adolescent words, maybe this was one of the reasons why Alex went for that *muy aggressivo* look: to differentiate himself from all the other seventeen-year-olds in Ralph Lauren Polo and blond curls like faggot archangels.

Anyway, the ice was definitely broken by the arguments about soccer, and in conformance with the theory of natural law, the discussion in Rinaldi's living room was drowned out by the usual topics: tits and asses and cunts and.

Old Alex was the oldest of the crew, even if by a few months, and Hoge and the master of the house knew each other well; so Alex knew he was going to have to deal with a salvo of pushy questions. And in fact Rinaldi had already turned to him with an air of total trust that could've been used with the accountant: "Hey, dude, so what do you think of that Tedeschi babe?"

The way Hoge snickered you could tell right off the bat that this was the hub around which heated and tortuous discussions revolved daily; a sort of semicollective enigma still unresolved. If he wanted to maintain the authority he'd always enjoyed, our tough guy had to give the right answer. Maybe some guys liked her and others didn't. From the way he asked, Rinaldi definitely liked her.

In the end, Alex smiled like an ancient good father who knows and shares his son's weaknesses: "Well, I'd say she's a more than fuckable Entity, the Tedeschi babe. Excellent ass, and even up front . . . Definitely, more than just fuckable." You could tell Rinaldi was going into ecstasy, he had one of those looks. But Hoge appeared more than skeptical. "Even the *face,*" Alex insisted. "Even the face is incredible. And you know sometimes blondes can be a little twatty, especially bleached blondes. But Tedeschi . . . I mean she's no twat."

There, he got even the half approval of old Hoge. "Look, trust me. Tedeschi is a way fuckable piece of ass. Fuckin' A, she's got some flawless shit on her. I mean she's perfect, like a blow-up doll!"

Rinaldi, spread out on the couch with his hands on his belly full of cookie crumbs, went into a recollection.

"Man, she was after me three years ago, remember?"

"Seriously? Shit, I'd still be kicking myself in the head."

"I am, I am. She was after me, don't you remember? I was a retard, no two ways about it."

"Now she's with that Mazzuoli guy in third year. The burnout with a red jacket."

"Yeah, but she's only with the burnout because he's got a car. *God,* when I think that she wanted my ass back then . . . Anyway, you wanna know why she's with Mazza? I'll tell you why. Because they're all whores, the chicks in our school. The worst kind of whores. *Nun*whores. They pretend to be nuns, and when they find some prick, I mean some real fucking prick, they become worse than those blondes on the street."

"Well, not all of them. Not Pastorelli."

"Man, but she's one fugly creature, horror-show fugly, I'm sorry. No way she'll ever be a nunwhore. She's just fugly. She'll never be a nunwhore."

"Yeah, right, but I'd do her just the same. Listen, they're all nunwhores anyway, even the fugly ones. You just put a bag over her head and fuck her with the lights out . . . They're all the same down there anyway."

"But then you're better off . . . I mean even jerking off is something. Man, you're better off choking the chicken."

"Nah, it's different when there's a whole body wiggling against you . . ."

"Yeah, but *Pastorelli's* body? I don't know. And if I couldn't get it up for the rest of my life?"

"Oh man, and what's that girl's name in your class, that real babe, with two big knockers, skinny . . . way fuckable . . ."

"Flavia Maria Ferri?"

"That's it. Flavia Maria."

"Shit, she's totally fuckable. She only goes with twenty-year-olds . . . I mean you're tellin' me about Flavia . . ."

"Why, cuz you guys think those huge dudes that pick her up from school are bangin' her?"

"I'd say she's already given them her urethra," old Alex threw in. "I mean her pisshole."

"We're gonna wind up getting arrested here," Hoge said. His vital signs weren't as strong as at the start. Every five minutes he took another sip and for a second seemed bummed. Rinaldi though was soaring through the forest of his imagination with all of Flavia Maria naked under the shower in a Mexican hotel, and him bursting in with a coconut in his hand.

"Sure ain't easy to get inside though."

"Here, don't think about it. Let's make another toast. To love."

"Right."

"More than right. To love."

"Man, in the movies you see people who meet in the afternoon and by nighttime they're giving it to each other every which way. Straight off. For *hours*. Never happens to us that way. I mean is it an age thing?"

"Age doesn't mean shit. It depends on the school. They're all wood-cunts, don't you see? They tease, tease, tease and won't give it up. At least not to us. They'll show it off, but won't put out. So you gotta really look around, see other worlds. Who knows, go to a Catholic school. Those Catholic school bitches learn how to give head when they're thirteen. Even my cousin Nando says so: Maria's daughters give it up like water. I have my own theory about girls, and my other cousin Pietro can confirm it: the ones who tease during the year and give you a platonic kiss on the mouth at max, when they're on vacation, especially at the beach, they *totally* let loose. All right. Hear me out on this. You think maybe they like the guys on the beach that much more? Or maybe in the city they hold out so they can look like prudes? *No way,* right? But my cousin Pietro from the beach swears it, and not just him, but other guys. He swears that all those tourist chicks just pounce on the beach in Rimini in a spastic hunt for cock. Then after they've had their fill, when they get back to Parma, Varese, Luganobello, Vicenza, Bergamo, Guastalla, Verona or wherever, y'know what they do? They burn the bridges with their beach boys, like they don't answer letters, don't return calls . . . They don't talk to you anymore. You're like dead for them. They raise a wall of polar ice, and what's done is done. You think that's right?"

No way.

Applause.

Vodka.

"All true. Sacrosanct. But look, it also has to do with the fact that we're here in Italy, you know? There're Countries and there're Countries, right? Rich Countries and poor Countries. In the poor ones they deal with it like that. I mean look at

Greece! Look at Portugal! Look at Africa! There's places where fifteen-year-olds have three kids already. Fifteen, fourteen years old and three kids already! And then there're Catholic Countries and non-Catholic Countries. In the Catholic countries the girls have a shitload of complexes, they're scared of being whores, or maybe they threaten you with equality—though not as much now, cuz they've figured out it's easier to stay home and do nothing. But anyway, they won't take cock even if you beg them on your knees. But look at the North! Look at Holland! Look at Sweden! Besides the fact that they're drop-dead gorgeous by the time they're fourteen. Here they've got braces and greasy hair . . . I don't know . . ."

"Like Zanardi's girlfriend."

"Yeah, but she's eighteen, not fourteen. Get it? It's not the same."

"All right, Zanardi's girlfriend is totally scuzzy. But you know what I'm saying. Go north of the Alps and you'll see."

Fuckin' A! Let's go!

Vodka!

"This summer my folks are sending me to college in Exeter," Hoge said. His wick was slowly burning down.

"Last year I was in London with a family. The lady of the house had two daughters, one our age and one a year younger."

"So now you're gonna tell us that you did all of them *together*. Please, *tell* me that's what happened!"

"Yeah right, even the mother . . . What, are you stupid or something? The older one used to bring these huge guys home. It was out of the question. But the other one, who seemed all sweet and fine and good, was so hard up for cock you couldn't stay next to her. Rita. Her name was Rita. Okay. So one fine day we were alone in the house. She was in her room, and I was in the living room watching TV. After a while she came down, and sat right next to me. Now, there were two huge couches in that living room, but the girl sits right next to me, almost on top of me, and she puts her arm over my shoulders . . ."

. . . Here's the thing that really bugged Alex: that his stories were *true*. Sure, at times he'd add a little color to some of the details, but he definitely wasn't one of those bullshit artists that you see around these days, trying to be cool at all costs. Only there was no way to tell the difference between the liar who swore he was sincere and the one who really was sincere. That's the thing that screws you, so you're better off telling true stories with a light heart and bullshit with minute details, no?

". . . So I didn't say a word. And wouldn't you know, she starts looking into my eyes like Bambi. She's right in front of me. *Three Amigos* was on the tube, and one of the phony gunslingers got to the point where the bush starts singing."

Okay, a cinematic shiver, let's give Alex credit for it. I mean to put a scene of domestic peace alongside a sex scene gives you the impression of someone who's shot his load contentedly and is almost distracted. And a lot of late adolescents go for that. And it serves its purpose.

Now, for example, Alex just finished shaping the fifteen-year-old Rita Wilson's hips with his hands in the air. How could a gesture like that, right there in old Rinaldi's living room, not hit home? There was no way it couldn't. Rinaldi's eyes were spinning like pinwheels, and his jaw was seriously dislocated . . . Hoge, on the other hand, was blank, spreading himself out over the couch under our eyes.

". . . So with *Three Amigos* at the talking bush scene, Rita Wilson starts taking off my shirt. And me, nothing. I'm immobile. I look at her without saying anything. But after a while I get up and start taking *her* clothes off . . ."

And here, late-adolescent Alex embraced his audience with his gaze—a real fighter-pilot nosedive straight for a pinpoint on the floor—while old Rinaldi, his jaw fractured by now, stood and stared at the ground, waiting for the almost sixteen-year-old Rita Wilson to materialize, sweating and whinnying right there on the rug in his living room . . .

". . . What else could I do at that point? I had to impale her on the spot, right there on the carpet. Afterwards, when she was taking a shower, I watched the end of *Three Amigos,* when they beat the Guapo men."

At times reality was wilder than any fantasy.

Old Alex.

All right, he didn't mention it there in the living room to Rinaldi and Hoge, but the story about the English fifteen-year-old was pretty much true, only it was no big thing. He remembered the place: Joan Armatrading and Lionel Richie albums piled up on the dresser, the sheer curtains, the beige carpet, a plate full of cookies on the floor.

"How the hell did you do it? I mean with precautions! How did you do it with those pain-in-the-ass precautions?"

Ah, the precautions, the precautions. Alex had a flashback of those more or less cold sweats he went through that anxious autumn.

"I used the quail jump method. There was no other way. The quail jump. Pull it out in time. There's your precaution. But if I can give you some advice, don't ever do anything stupid, cuz kids here are dropping into the world like grapes off a vine, and you gotta be careful as a cougar."

"You're telling me? I always keep a rubber on me."

Old Hoge got some life back into him.

It was probably the same one for years. The rubber, I mean.

"Sure, but to break in ain't so easy. You need a little *el blow* grease. Otherwise you're stuck outside."

That was the golden age Rinaldi talking. An immortal. It was Rinaldi who ogled the films with Edwige Fenech and Alvaro Vitali behind his folks' backs. He had to go to the furthest newspaper stand to get hold of those discount porno flicks so as not to risk running into any of his relatives.

Only now that Alex had gotten him all hot and horny, Rinaldi insisted on all of them watching *Hot Policewomen's Alcatraz Mission,* at least. Now. There. At his house. Not that Alex was all that into it, but still, seeing as how Hoge, all tanked on vodka, didn't even want to hear about turning back, and old Rinaldi already had the video in his hand after having uprooted it from a bookshelf, and it was half out of its case marked *Red Hot Chili Peppers Live in Holland,* alias title impenetrable enough to keep his family units at a distance . . . What else was there to do at this point? You had to humor him and watch.

The time dripped into quarter to eleven.

By twelve twenty the hot policewomen had already accepted and inserted miles of cock, the ice cold vodka was finished, and old Alex felt a brash sandman making his way up from some interior shadow zone.

Finally it was time to go back home. Monday . . . Yes, Monday five o'clock . . . Alex had to be home between one fifteen and one thirty.

He absolutely had to get himself together, and *now*.

The time came for all the bye Rinaldi, bye old boy, yo don't call me Rinaldi call me Rocco, cool, bye Rocco, bye old boy, later Hoge, sorry man I left my bag, later Alex, see ya dude, did I have a jacket?

Comic laughter.

Then Alex went down the stairs with a somewhat unreal lightness, while Hoge couldn't manage to walk a straight line and nearly banged into every poor shop on Rinaldi's street, the poor paper shop, the poor dry cleaner, even the poor guy working on the water pipes . . . What the hell was up with Rinaldi's street that everyone was so poor?

It was incredible for old Hoge. Who knows how Rinaldi felt when everyone talked about their summer vacations here and there, and he, at max, went to his grandmother's house up in the mountains? Old Hoge couldn't walk a straight line, but still he asked himself these questions.

They found a half-empty bus going downtown, and they horsed around the whole time they were on the bus. Then, seeing as how old Hoge was just a stop away, they said good-bye in the usual manner, with the old homeboy handshake. One last hug, another laugh, and Alex was alone, with the vodka swirling and a headache that was assuming generational proportions.

A terrible struggle with himself to get off where he could change for the 20, then cross the street and reach the stop where he could actually get on the 20, de facto.

After an indeterminate period of time had elapsed, he zeroed in on the orange whale coming toward him down a straight stretch, pitching back and forth. It finally stopped to open its useless black rubber maw in front of him. Get on. Climb in, calmly. It was hot as hell with hordes of sweaty people in the bus, shit. (Okay. I'm totally blitzed. Totally, okay . . . the vodka . . . swimming in the sauce. All right. Tanked to the max.) And then there was this one parochial-type lady with blue hair and a poodle fur, who said to him: "'Scuse me, young man . . . ," and old Alex was staying up by hugging the ticket validator, and a hushed little voice in his vodka-soaked brain was saying: "You're cool. Just get on your feet and move. Just get on your feet and move."

"Young man, can y'hear me? 'Scuse me."

On your *feet? Move?* Impossible! With all that booze swirling through his brain cells? Impossible!

Then Alex looked at the poodle's blue hair, but couldn't understand a thing. "Let's not collapse now, all right? Let's not make an ass of ourselves," said the voice swimming through the vodka in his brain. At one point he made an incredible effort to smile at the blue poodle and saw her expression was all neorealistic and realized he was smiling at her like some poor earthquake victim at the National Guardsman standing in front of the rubble of his house with his two deaf-mute kids beside him.

Okay. Old Alex watched all of via Farini and piazza Cavour go by in slow-mo. He'd never get home, he knew it. Or maybe he'd get there in five or six hours. That is, *real slow.*

And the old farts in the bus would rip him to pieces like in *A Clockwork Orange,* when twenty or thirty old veiny hairy hands grab the handsome and dazzling teenager and massacre him, tearing his hair out and the rest of him apart. And they ripped him to pieces out of envy, because they were eternally damned to be old, and he wasn't. He was crazy and young.

Voices came to him from the owners of veiny hairy hands. Some came from underwater, naturally, but on the whole they came from behind, in the back of the bus. The voices had something against young junkies, no doubt. And the only young junkie around, the only addict strung out against the ticket validator holding him up was him—so fuck you, assholes.

Then came a husky hoary underwater voice—Alex couldn't see him underwater, obviously, but sure enough the hoary guy must've had one of those bald heads where the long hairs of one side were transported to the other to cover the bald patch. The husky hoary guy couldn't stand all the Lowlifes and Debauchery. When he was young, there were no lowlifes in Bologna. In his youth there was no debauchery. "Like *débauche* in French," Alex thought. "Why not? Debauchery, *la débauche* . . ." He was doubled over and managed to see the tips of his shoes through the sauce. Then, something about the trains that used to be on time. Beautiful.

Outside there was already a little of the zoo, a little circus: all the fourteen-year-olds on via D'Azeglio on their new scooters and the little chicks starting to whore around. Skateboard helmets, sneakers . . .

Trains hazy with sweat on time.

Another underwater voice: "'Scuse me, young man, but I have to validate my ticket."

"Leave him be. The poor boy's sick."

Drugs. Debauchery.

"You're all pricks. I'm going home to eat. And I don't remember inviting you all."

"If you're sick, maybe you should go to the hospital!"

"Just ain't right. *First* they do what they please, *then* hassle everyone else."

"Poor boy, I feel sorry for him. Me, who's a mother."

"Only a mother can know the pain . . ."

"Yeah, yeah, but I have to punch my ticket. What if the controller comes?"

Didn't they know that Alex had thousands of gnomes stuck to his hairs and they were chipping away at his head with thousands of mallets and chisels? Then the husky hoary guy decided to abandon the depths of the abyss and manifested himself in all his spastic glory, and the old ladies swimming around him must've thought he was pretty brave in the end; and the backs of some of the menopausal hags there must've felt the rush of indomitable shivers, like little sixteen-year-old beavers when Tom Cruise flattens some scumbag mugger with his bare hands, no?

Short with retreating hairline. Sideburns the color of a gun barrel. Over sixty. On the road to rage.

"Ooh," Alex thought, still hugging the ticket validator. "Oof, now he's gonna hit me, a punch to the gut and I'm gonna drop like a lead zeppelin and split my head open: not righteous, though, to take advantage of my state," he added to himself.

The husky guy wore a mush-colored weekday suit. A bleu sweater, as they say in Bolognese, peered out from under his jacket. "Pardon me, young man, but there's a crowd of people here that want to punch their tickets. They have a right to do that, no?"

Ooh. Firm, but gentle.

"Look, you're firm but gentle," old Alex wheezed while the gnomes pummeled him with their mallets, and his face flushed in the sun.

He must've come across like a total nutjob with that death wheeze.

"You're bothering a whole crowd of people, young man. Please move aside."

Ooh.

"Listen," Alex reflected. "You remind me of this song . . ." Ooh. ". . . 'Don't know what I want, but I know how to get it. And I wanna destroy if I can . . .' It's an old song. A song you can dance to. It's called 'Anarchy in Italy.' You know it?"

And with that, the choir of old ladies that seemed in a hazy way to be near his grandmother's house, started up again with their "Oh, he's so young . . ." and "Poor thing, we should call the Red Cross," while the matronlike voices sewn in somewhere between the back entrance and the last row of seats echoed with "Yes, they start so young. Of course, they have everything!" and with "The *police,* call them, not the Red Cross!"

Alex smiled again in that same burnt-out, neorealistic way as before, and the husky guy in front of him hadn't yet decided whether he should laugh or flatten him with a shot to the solar plexus. Inside, the bus was immersed in a flux of indecision, and the world outside turned at the intersection of the little streets and via Saragozza, and old Alex was push-parked by invisible hands into a seat left free by a charitable and well-kept house-wife, the kind that spend lots of time at the hairdresser.

Because today's woman—as Alex, slouched in his seat, re-flected—always needs more attention paid to herself, to feel connected to her man. This afternoon it'll rain

bullshit.

By now he was chill

out.

Off.

From the magnetic archive of Mr. Alex D. I have two balls that only I know about. Anyway I would like to let whoever the hell will listen to this cas-sette in the year 3000 know that the famous adoles-cence included such afternoons, notwithstanding the fact that in 3000 there will still be adolescents with I-don't-give-a-shit attitudes and parents who won't know why.

I don't give a shit. It happens often in this season when you wake up and the sky is grayish white, and at noon the sky is grayish white, and in the evening the sky is grayish white, and maybe even at night, behind the blinds, the gray is always there looking at you, always the same, like it was six in

the afternoon for life, from the time you wake up to
the time you go to sleep totally pissed off because
you've been out of step the whole time.

Anyway, besides summer, the rest of the year is
almost always like this for me. So I go on my bike
instead of on the bus, because at least by pedaling
in a cold that freezes the sparrows on the branches
you feel alive. At least you feel like you're doing
something a little weird, solitary, even heroic.

I'm here, Tuesday afternoon, splayed out on the
bed, belly up; totally vegged out under the giant
pictures of Malcolm X and the Pistols, listening to
the Splatter Pink demo my friend Hoge lent me. I
haven't studied for tomorrow. I'm pounding my head
with a shovel and all these guilt trips are jumping
out like moles from every opening.

I hear the Matron talking in her usual anxious
tone over the telephone. Surely it's the Chancellor
at the other end of the line. And surely they're talking about Mr. Alex D. But it doesn't matter if I can
hear what they say.

Same old same old. He's wasting himself. He's
throwing himself away. He never does anything. And
lately, and so on.

I run my hand across my calf with my eyes closed.
I feel the roughness of the hair.

You can barely make out the words in the Splatter
Pink demo. The bass player, D. D. Bombay, is totally
manic, like all the rest of the hard-core bass players.

It'd be nice to have the American lyric sheet.
If I were him I'd write my name Dee Dee Bombay, same
with Chuck Dee of Public Enemy.

The graphics on the inside booklet are pretty
shitty. The photos, even though they're sharp, are
too nebulous to really give you an idea of the band
onstage . . .

(. . . It's better to choose from the beginning who
will really stay with you. Choosing individuals who
will spit in your face is your prerogative, but you
can't come to me and say it's all their fault. We're
divided. Too many assholes between us, and you know
it. Isolating yourself can help in discovering who's
malignant among us. There's always someone ready to
sympathize with your cause, then one day you find
out they're worse than the rest. You see them accept
what they refused in the beginning . . .)

Dee Dee Bombay
Maybe old Dee Dee would consider Martino a
wretched asshole. Because of his social class, and
his I-don't-give-a-shit-ism. Maybe Dee Dee would tell
me to isolate myself . . .
I sure am isolated in school though. Isolated
with my little crew of red catholic punks. We don't
even try to mix with the others. Wussies with the
wussies and red catholic punks with the red catholic
punks, good god . . .

Enrico Brizzi

"You think you're all *better* than everyone else?"
the more liberal and daring ones ask. No, what are
you saying? Not at all. But we believe we're different from most of the zombie students at Caimani. And
this, hell yes. We don't think we're better, but we're
sure we've made the only choice possible, or at least
the most coherent. We don't care about the teachers'
mafialike warnings. We try to make others respect
us, as much as that's possible; and try to explain
to the teachers that they can't tell us about matu-
rity when they never even show up at the assemblies,
or when in order to keep students in line they pass
by the seats and confiscate books that aren't strictly
necessary for their subject and try to get attention
with ultradiscipline rather than with lessons that
are a little interesting · · ·

They look at you cross if they find out you're
reading for your own head. Or if you open your eyes,
or leave the herd. I don't want anything to do with
these shitty people. I don't want to be their accom-
plice, I don't want to be their friend. They can take
their dickhead irony and their scholastic programs
and stick them firmly where the sun don't shine.

In their game, me and my friends are lost pawns,
irrecoverable·

No, we don't think we're better· Surely my parents will reproach me, because they say I'm a trouble-
maker, and they consider my friends, on the average,
to be nothing but huge pricks, because we could just

shut up and get our passing grades with no effort instead of causing problems.

Rinaldi and Martino wouldn't approve, but I think yours truly should follow the advice of old Dee Dee Bombay.

I'm too tired to compromise.

Or maybe I'm just too tired.

Okay. Cinematic shiver. An afternoon much grayer and more varnished with headaches than the others came along. One of those afternoons spent studying for ten minutes, getting up with every new paragraph to shoot a mainline of MTV, wait for the next video, if it sucks I split, if it's cool I stay . . .

In the end, Alex stayed in front of the tube for hours, because there was no way he could deal with closing himself in his room with the Pantheist Spinoza and the Skeptic Hume all underlined by the previous owner of *Philosophy and Philosophers in History,* as rocky and shattered as he was.

Then, the telephone. It wasn't the Chancellor calling from Rome to find out if everything was going well and the family was keeping busy and healthy.

Matter of fact, it was Aidi.

He'd been waiting for the call for a while, but he didn't know what to say . . .

(The essential is invisible to the eye, said the fox.)

"Hi, Alex . . . I got your letter. How are you, really?"

"Really?"

"Yeah, how are you?"

"Bad, Aidi. How the hell should I be, if not bad?"

"..."

He listened to her breathe.

"I wanted . . . I'd like to start seeing each other. There, I said it."

Okay. Now he was *glad.* But would it do any good?

Okay, it was cool. Had to try. Had to try and that was that, because just seeing her gave him joy, just brushing up against her and looking at her with those undertones in his eyes.

"Alex?"

"You hurt me, Aidi." Ooh. "You hurt me bad. And I missed you . . ." Ooh. "I thought it was all over with, but I knew that wasn't possible. Because you're"—forgive him forgive him forgive him—"*different* from all the other girls I've met . . . When we'd run into each other in the halls, in school, I knew you were acting; when you'd pass by without stopping to talk, I knew and you knew. Why'd you do that?"

"I'm sorry. I swear I'm not saying it just to say it, I swear this is how I feel one hundred percent. I realize I was real stupid. There . . . But I didn't do it to hurt you. Do you believe me?"

"..."

"*Alex,* do you *believe* me?"

"What should I say? I believe you didn't do it to hurt me on purpose, if that's what you tell me. I just want to understand what the whole thing means, or meant. Not answering me that night, not calling me, acting as if I didn't exist . . ."

"Because I was scared, I swear . . . I did all of it for both of us. Alex . . . I don't feel like being together with you . . ."

"Look, I understood as much within a minute of asking you." Ooh.

75

"Don't misunderstand me, please. I don't feel like being together with *anyone*. I don't feel like getting tied down to someone and creating a kind of closed world where you can't let anyone in . . ."

"All right, Aidi."

"But what I wanted to tell you, listen to me please, is that I want to see you, hang out, go out. I realized it was weird with you . . . I don't feel like being together, but in some ways we're beyond being together. I feel you inside, Alex. I understand you, and I like you . . ."

Great. Just shoot me, riddle me with bullets, right here. Thank you. Like Sid Vicious's "My Way." Fire whenever you like.

". . . Aidi, I swear I was a total basket case. I got into all those horrible head trips like he just got dumped by a girl and doesn't want to study and gets no satisfaction from school and has lots of friends but the sincere ones you can confide in are so rare. He's got no goals in life. Being happy, maybe, but he's a long way off from even the *idea* of it. And everything around him is just the same old stuff, and maybe it'll always be like that too. Everything is so predictable, and I've already lived in a hundred films, all the same, and I feel like a character in a book I don't like, and I hate the author that makes me do these things I hate, all these things that don't make me feel the least bit happy and . . ."

Okay. We think she should stop him, before it's too late. Anyway, forgive him. As a matter of fact, don't even listen to me. Just fire and that'll be that.

". . . Alex, but this is just what I wanted to tell you. I think us two, in some way, I don't know, we could break out of the book. I feel guilty for all that's happened these past few days, and I wanted to tell you right away, but I was too scared you wouldn't want anything to do with me, with us . . ."

"No way. Shit. Even if we're not together, it's no problem. What we both gotta do now is find a place outside the book."

Like on Uranus.

"Are you into going out Saturday night? We could talk, or do whatever we feel like."

She was going for it. She was going for it.

"Aidi, I'm cool just talking. Or even sitting on your windowsill, holding hands and staring at the sky."

You bet.

"Really? I'm glad, Alex. I swear I'm not just saying it to say it."

That's clear.

"I'm glad too, Aidi, real tired and real glad. I wish tomorrow was Saturday, but instead it's just a ball-busting Thursday at school."

True grit.

"Like the fox says to the little prince, 'When I'm an hour away from meeting you, I'll start to be happy, and get more and more restless . . .'"

"I hope Saturday comes in a hurry too."

And then they were quiet with the receivers in their hands for at least half a minute, listening to each other breathe and smile.

"... Aidi?"

"Yes?"

"Tomorrow, at school, when we see each other, run up to me, please. All these days I've been hoping for that, but it never happened . . ."

Okay. *Fire!*

"All right, Alex."

"Promise?"

"Sure. I promise."

"I'm happy, Aidi. Now I'm gonna go to sleep, and it'll be like a dream."

"A sweet dream?"

That's *clear.*

"... Beautiful. Bye, Aidi."

"Hey, Alex."

"Yeah."

"I like you a lot."

Ooh.

Second

Adelaide's house was in the seminary's park

Adelaide's house was in the seminary's park, on a hill, outside of porta San Mamolo. To get there you had to climb up via Codivilla, which was one of those places Alex would never take a baby in a buggy ride.

Not that he normally went for walks with babies, but if for some reason the buggy got away from him and rolled down the steep hill at a hundred miles an hour in a screaming streak and smashed into pieces against a tree or the front of a car, he felt that right then and there, he wouldn't have been able to keep from thinking about the luckless Fantozzi character in all those sad movies.

It made him shudder, the Fantozzi thing.

I mean like a hysterical reaction.

Anyhow, those strange days went by and not even the shadow of Martino, no phone call, nothing. There was the increasing possibility that he wouldn't be able to graduate. At least those were the rumors. But Martino was nowhere to be found in the school hallways, and Alex wasn't too worried about looking for him, because those were very late-adolescent days, and let's just say his afternoons were more and more booked up

he got to Aidi's house around six, six thirty. They stayed together about an hour, on the veranda, or in the room, or sometimes hidden in the tall meadow grass, lying on their backs looking at the white streaks of airplanes flying between Moscow and New York. That helluva guy got hornier lying in the grass beside Adelaide, holding her hand, than he had in all the sporadic Particularly Erotic Moments of his life. It was all so new, clean, fresh, he thought. Something a little from a book, he thought. With her departure date already set, unfortunately, and despite not having a clear outline of the separation that lay ahead, he couldn't manage to set fire to that feeling of nostalgia. There'd be time in the future to learn those blues riffs, okay, he wasn't *that* stupid, and he'd known it back then already. But he tried to think about all that as little as possible

(Aidi's exes. Alex's exes.)

it struck him as strange and intriguing, the fact that they wouldn't really be together . . .

Anyway, that helluva guy had fun talking with no hangups about all the girls he kind of liked and was interested in and so on. But when she talked about guys, he always took it to heart. As long as she was just talking about how this guy or that guy was *cute,* he was fairly cool about it, but when he imagined that she could actually be together with one of those guys, he realized that their—my God—*relationship* would have been dealt a mortal blow. That said, for his part Alex was quite able to reconcile the two demands though: Aidi and *all* the other eventual girls.

Well, at least they talked about it, hidden in the high grass.

* * *

"Maybe you just want to stay with me, and so you have to think about other girls so as not to hurt your pride, to show yourself that you could get it on with this, that and the other one . . ."

"Maybe you're right," old Alex, the immortal rock, had to agree. They continued to make goo-goo eyes at each other from a hand's breadth away, then changed the topic. They laughed, got serious, then went back to little waves of giggles until he had to jump on his bike and fly back home. Usually, when he was about to leave, Aidi's mother showed up in her little red car with Federico—Aidi's blond little brother, fresh out of some day-care center. Her mother was very nice, and he seriously admired her for having raised the family on her own.

(It seemed to Alex that she found him nice, or something like that.)

Federico had a plastic gun that shot yellow, cone-shaped darts at a square target with points marked on it. He was pretty good, even if he had a hard time loading it. When Federico would be their age, sixteen or seventeen, Aidi and her sister Chiara would by then be way past the juvenile world of pizzerias, concerts and college, Alex thought. Who knew if Alex and the kid would still see each other? For now he brought him comic books, and read to him occasionally for just a minute or two.

Then there was always the fact that he never interacted physically with Aidi—not even a kiss on the mouth! But apart from that, Aidi always wore those prodigious white T-shirts and listened to soft rock like the Housemartins or some Italian singers from the seventies. They also played cards and Pic-Up Stix together.

Alex always lost—perennially restless, anxious and tormented as he was. You could hardly win at Pic-Up Stix in such a state.

And then they talked and talked. They talked about things they never mentioned to anyone—afternoons lying on the rug, or sitting in the courtyard, talking about past summers and fears for the future. Alex kept repeating that at the end of June, when they were supposed to say good-bye to each other, he'd be sad. Aidi smiled without saying anything.

He was a bit disappointed that she didn't say she would be terribly sorry not to see him for a whole year—but the disappointment only lasted for a second. Our helluva guy would raise his eyes and there she was again, adjectiveless Aidi.

They even stayed silent once in a while. Hugging on the bed, their breath going up and down. (They were the slowest, damnedest, most intense silences Alex had ever heard.)

Sometimes he'd go to her house after dinner. A few times he had to blow off his ex-boyscout buddies in order to go to her house, then regretted it a bit.

(He only talked about Aidi with his closest rocker friends.)

Usually, at this time, Federico was asleep and Aidi's mother was upstairs watching TV. In any case, they couldn't make noise. The two of them would light a candle and put it on the kitchen table, letting a little wax drip onto the plate to hold it tight.

During the more paranoid evenings they plunged themselves headlong into conversations about their relationship, how
it was different from just friendship, or any other feeling they
could find words for.

(Our tough guy always wound up feeling bad.)

During the brighter evenings, however, they flew well together, like in certain extraordinary novels. They talked about
Holden Caulfield and old Jane, and they were radiant as they
held hands.

On those spring evenings, sitting at the kitchen table with
books scattered about, the music low and the candle lit, Alex
began to understand what happiness was. And maybe he even saw
that other dart-throwing demigod running swift and silent as
a shadow, just out the window. It seemed to be him all right.
Indeed, thinking about it with a few months' hindsight, he would
be convinced beyond a doubt. Ooh, it was him. Definitely . . .

(In the light of that ominous candle, he felt the immense power
we have within us for the first time.)

Looking at her lips in silence, her hair, her hands in the candle-
light, made him feel majestic, like lying down on the tracks and
stopping a locomotive with the strength of his legs, or swimming
breathlessly for hours in a sea of—forgive him—*peach flavored
tea*. He was Shane MacGowan, the holy hard-drinking punk
poet looking out the window of a train at the last cars following
him without ever catching him.

But all this stuff Alex would realize only later, because in those days all he felt was that ominous mix of happiness and anxiety which he'd never felt before. Aidi was like a luminous fairy, a flawless Entity, the Sunny Side of the Street, the voice of Shane with the music of the Pogues. It was their favorite kabbala: I just wanna stay right there, on the sunny side of the street.

Aidi said that when they listened to it, old Alex's eyes shined, you'll see.

One morning they got together at quarter to eight by porta San Mamolo and he gave her a pack of fluorescent star stickers as a gift. In the afternoon they'd stick them on the closet by her bed in the form of—forgive him, then shoot him—zodiac constellations, Scorpio and Pisces. That lump of cycling muscles pedaled at top speed, and she followed behind him on her scooter. She laughed and said he looked funny when he stood up on his bike along the disconnected cobblestones of via d'Azeglio.

One afternoon in March, at Feltrinelli's bookstore, Alex passed by the display of new novels and paperbacks, then bought a book with black and white photos of the Clash from '77 to the Grand Finale. Meanwhile she spent the whole time reading a book on Buddhism. While they strolled around the downtown area under a carbon monoxide sun, Aidi explained to him how Zen monks would sometimes spend years trying to find the answer to a single koan. Our helluva guy, on the other hand, went on about how Joe Strummer chose the punk singer trip even if his father was some bigwig British diplomat. Then Adelaide told him about where she came from, Sicily, with such intensity and sincerity that he could never forget it. She owned at least ten books about the Mafia. But apart from that—apart from the trials, the boy judges and that film about the Sicilian transvestite in prison—it was the way she waxed poetic when describing the countryside, the sea and the volcanoes that seduced him. It was like he could smell it all even when he was pedaling like mad down an avenue full of exhaust fumes. All in all he thought about it as a fortunate land. Passionate. By now it was decided: sooner or later he'd have to see it.

During the course of those days, it was like he finally managed to grasp the strange lyrics from that Beatles song: "Happiness is a warm gun," which up to that point had always seemed like some sort of picturesque metaphor or a good slogan for an advertising campaign.

It electrified him, the certainty that if he or Aidi had gotten together with someone, everything would've fallen back into the book again, back into the hard garage rock, raw and kicking, the way he liked to listen to it up until two months ago. Still Alex really needed things to go ahead like this for a while. Just a little while longer and what came before would never come back. Just a little more time being happy like this, and he'd be catapulted out from the book forever.

Just a while longer playing Pic-Up Stix with her and he'd manage to send any future Alex-Chancellor to the mat. Till the end of June like this. Emotional anarchy until she leaves, and then, whatever happens, nothing will be as it was before.

If nothing could separate them up till the moment of her departure, it would be like Richie Cunningham becoming the president of the United States, or like playing the intro to "Foxey Lady" with the Stratocaster in flames just like the intro on old Jimi's album.

Yes, our helluva guy would've believed it.

He would've believed it every day and always.

He watched the old man with gray wool jacket amble toward the dark area of the confessional until the little green light over the doorframe went out and in its place a red warning light appeared: the sign "Father Fortunato" trembled with cyberpunk shivers imbued with the reflection of the new purplish light. Then, the old man in gray jacket's voice muttered something behind the door, slightly ajar, mixing with the hum of the ventilators. Alex made out only a carrion of syllables or consonant knots, and, at intervals, a bit of a donkey cough emitted from the confessional's belly. Then even the carrion of syllables ceased. The senior citizen with gray wool jacket peered out from behind the creaking door and streaked along the perimeter of the nave, leaving the coast clear.

Inside the confessional, Father Fortunato's breath floated in its own human all too human way. Furious aromas. Old Alex had just turned his back to the nave—reassuring himself that the door was ajar—which was filled to the brim with senior citizens singing the communion hymn, and with a single glance deemed worthy the half dozen editions of the Act of Contrition that permeated the semidarkness.

"Praise be to Jesus Christ, my son."

"Praise be forever."

Alex caught a glimpse of Father Fortunato's monkish face

through the holes in the form of a cross which adorned the metal screen and allowed the communication between souls. "It'd be simpler to talk about some things if there wasn't anything between us souls and the confessor," Alex thought.

"So, how are we?"

Father Fortunato's breath was at times overwhelming.

"Pretty well, I'd say."

From the magnetic archive of Mr. Alex D. This is one of my favorite paranoia trips: for a couple of years, every time I enter a confession booth I feel giddy, euphoric, brilliant. A whole bunch of things come to my mind, most of them practical jokes I do to the priests closed in their little cages, like dressing up as a monkey or letting some animal loose.

To get myself together when such inebriating ideas come to mind, I try to think about things like massacre scenes, battlefields, officers in agony; but I've wound up conditioning myself to such an extent that now I only think of one thing (it's like having a movie projector in your brain that shoots the images onto a wall inside your skull, behind your forehead): a Union soldier seriously wounded, lying on his stomach with white gloves, suspenders over his blue uniform, ruffled hair and about a ten-day beard. He's got a yellow handkerchief around his neck and his eyes are half-closed. It's one of my most-recurring

images. Maybe it was a comic strip that I read when
I was a kid. Or maybe, but less likely, it was a
frame from a movie.

"When was the last time you confessed?"

"Uh. Two months ago. Maybe four." He wasn't lying consciously.

"So, what do you have to tell me?"

"Uh, I'd say things are pretty good. I don't think I've committed any particularly heinous sin. Sure, with the family and all I haven't been that helpful. I hardly ever help out, I think. Well, as a matter of fact, I never help the family out. At times I wasn't patient enough with my little brother—like when he asked me to help him with his homework and all. I told him that since I had to do my own, he could do his by himself. I mean, that seems right. But maybe I could've been a little nicer. And then a little practical joke from time to time. Which might seem harsh to whoever had to go through it . . . Even me, if I had to go through it, it would've been harsh. Yeah but . . . Just a few noogies, you know, and some smacks upside his head. Just kidding around stuff. I wanted to ask you something though . . ."

Father Fortunato was still there, unshakable, in three-quarter pose—his right hand was on his chest, lapping his long beard—quite possibly dead.

". . . Well, I don't know if the Bible ever talks about it anywhere. Maybe in the Old Testament, like in the Psalms . . . I don't know, but it's like, lately, this last week I mean, like . . . I don't know, like everything's getting *better and better*. Like I'm more myself. I'm taking full advantage of some potential that up to now I've only used a part of. Does it say anything about that, in the Bible I mean, in some saying or whatever? Like how at times everything seems to go well?"

He threw out the sentence with an excited tone, like a teenager trying to explain to a policeman a crime that happened in front of his eyes. He realized he came across as a delirious madman, but it didn't matter.

Father Fortunato, unshakable.

Seconds, *minutes,* maybe.

No tension.

Old Alex could've stolen away from the confession booth like a leopard and Father Fortunato wouldn't have batted an eyelid. Outside now, there was the communion silence, women with scarves over their head—"A sign of respect," the Matron always repeated when he was a kid—swarming up the nave and side aisles, the toddlers in shorts and wool jackets—"It's cold in the church"—embellished with navy decorations like life jackets or dolphins, champing at the bit to get on line too, while a dog's stentorian bark from the back made an infant scream. In the distance, the echoes of "Amen," each with a timbre and tone distinct from the one before, kept in rhythm by the professional whispers of the celebrants.

Alex ventured a slight cough.

Maybe the monk was moving his *eyelids?* It was somewhat of a paradoxical situation, no doubt.

And in the end.

"Very good, my son. The Bible doesn't really speak about it specifically. But it's a spirit which prevails throughout the

Bible, its unifying breath. Happiness, improvement. The prophets speak of it, even Jesus speaks of it . . ."

Okay. These pettifogger's devices didn't really uplift old Alex; he wanted to ask *when* the prophets spoke about it, and *when* Jesus did, because maybe Father Fortunato was making it all up. But faced with the specter of a moment's pause for ecstatic reflection, he let it go and that was that.

Off. He got to thinking about the soccer championship, a tournament he was losing interest in right before his eyes. As a kid though he used to follow it every Sunday. Now he didn't even know who was in first place. Every once in a while his brother, a die-hard fan, would tell him about what happened and give him profiles of the champions, even if the Chancellor never let them go to the games "because the stadiums are dangerous." But these tidbits of information were quite sparse, shreds of questions which were now beyond his interest.

Then, a sentence pronounced in a less mortal than usual tone forced him to interrupt his digressions: ". . . All right then, *carry on.* Let's continue like this. We're doing well, but keep in mind that faith must be lived together; that faith, alone, doesn't work; indeed, faith cannot exist by itself. Christ said that wherever two or more gather in His name, He would be present. The same with the family. The same with school. The same with work. And also every time the church group acts . . . Very well, my son. For penance, say three Hail Marys to the Madonna."

Old Alex was expecting it.

When he was a kid he had to say two Hail Marys, but around the time he turned thirteen, when he discovered he was

committing impure acts and referred it to a competent Authority, the duo became a trio in order to steer him away from the
dreaded autoeroticism.

"And now, recite the Act of Contrition, my son."

(One time, countless years ago, old Alex had forgotten the Act
of Contrition, and all he could do was burst into tears inside the
confessional.)

". . . Thus I absolve you of all your sins, in the name of the Father, the Son and the Holy Spirit."

"Well, thanks then. Good-bye."

"Good-bye to you, my son. And thank you for coming.
And a good Sunday to your family as well."

"Yes. Thank you, Father. Good-bye."

"Thank you, my son. And a good Sunday to you too."

"OK."

The crowd was now dispersing, and a deacon with strictly
lateral hair was announcing the usual notices about future
parochial events and activities. Old Alex stopped for a second
with his luminous forehead and turned to the altar, the Hail
Marys rolling around semiautomatically inside him.

Then, once on the bike, he went straight home like some
slightly shorter and grungier Girardengo, pedaling smoothly
through the wide beautiful black asphalt streets. Alex felt his
mood brighten.

The Matron would bring the tagliatelle with prosciutto
and peas in a cream sauce, veal cutlets and carrot cake to the

table, and at three sharp he'd break the finish line climbing via Codivilla and see the resplendent Aidi.

The air was chilly, and that latter-day Girardengo had his sleeves rolled up and a pair of majestic Pogues tunes in his head.

Two hours later Alex is back in the saddle again, pedaling ecstatically in an afternoon light that reminded him for a second of a few rare late afternoons in August, clear and blue like after a rain; one of those rare August days in Bologna she wouldn't see this year.

Meanwhile with the bike it got better and better. His strength had increased since he started going up via Codivilla.

The first time, he got halfway up the hill and his breath suddenly gave out on him. He had to get off and walk the bike up to the gate. It was evening over the hills, a thick pasty darkness. March, and out of the 8:30 P.M. blackness he got a whiff of spring coming.

The first few times, Aidi got off her scooter and waited for him at the gate. Alex remembered her sitting on the scooter, smiling with her helmet in her hands. Then Alex locked the bike up and rode with her to the house by the seminary. She rode well, even if last year she'd had an accident in Sicily. Old Alex couldn't avoid feeling sorry for that little accident months back, though it finished in the best way possible, and he couldn't have prevented it anyway.

Spring was slipping out of his hands, no doubt, but in the meantime he'd learn how to go with the changes, use his strengths well. He managed to get to the yard in front of the house before Aidi's without stopping.

He flew like a speeding bullet down the avenues, turning right on via San Mamolo, then, if there wasn't any traffic by the ice cream stand, he would turn into via Codivilla, shooting in like nobody. On the flat stretch he pedaled at top speed, then hit the hill with all his might under the surprisingly indifferent eyes of the rare pedestrians and drivers coming down the hill toward him, anesthetized, to get to the city. He tried to keep it in the same gear he used on the flat stretch, with the long stride covering more of the road, as far as it was possible; then he got up and pedaled on his feet, the whole bike dancing beneath him. When he felt the hill getting too steep and realized that after another pedal or two he'd have to put his feet on the ground, along the curve, usually after the first no parking sign, he hit the shift with his thumb and changed gears; the chain jumped to the smaller sprocket and his legs were pumping again; he moved himself along the curve, at the edge of the asphalt, up to the curb to avoid any unnecessary piece of road. Once out of the curve he was again able to pedal sitting down.

When he caught sight of the line of cars, he established a finish line he could cross without leaving his seat: at least up to the white VW—forearms tensed, back curved, veins on his hands and wrists visible, palms sweating.

At least up to that goddam Rabbit . . .

He thought about something else, looked at the ground in those difficult moments: the titles of Police albums. *Regatta De Blanc, Outlandos D'Amour, Synchronicity, Zenyatta Mondatta,*

Ghost in the Machine. Because *Regatta De Blanc* is before *Out-landos D'Amour,* right?

Old Alex mentally scanned the parked cars so as not to think about his body, which pedaled by itself anyway. He recognized almost all of them, even if here and there he couldn't remember the names of certain models, like those small Japanese ones.

Wh-wh-wh-ite R-r-r-abbit! On your feet now!

And now he was riding like the immortal Coppi. He pedaled on his feet, leaning forward, jutting out past the handlebars while the sweat dripped across his eyebrows and down behind his ears. His shirt was stuck to his back. Still a few yards to go, just a few yards and he'd catch sight of the two stone lions with their spent look, half asleep on top of the columns the gate was hinged to.

That huge gate with two totally indifferent, half-asleep lions was always open, and old Alex flew past it through the clean cool air of the trees. There was a flat stretch, inside, but he knew he shouldn't fool himself because if he slowed down to catch his breath on that piece, he'd hurt himself right afterwards trying to get his rhythm back; so he stood up for the asphalt curves that traversed the forest, and at the second curve, which turned to the right, he switched gears, the chain jumping onto the bigger sprocket. He shot up the hill off the straightaway standing on his feet again.

He shifted his back a little to stay on the outside of the curve, and now he was just a short piece of road away, before the seminary. He stayed on the flat gear. He could stop thinking about Coppi and Girardengo, and other legendary cyclists

and climbers with their thighs of iron and Nietzschean will—
destined to remain unknown, though with Girardengo they
came to him in all the mountain stages as he put the gym-bred
champions to shame.

Aidi was sixty seconds away.

The last few pumps to get to the yard in front of the
seminary.

Old Alex ran his hands through his soaking hair.

Ten pedals more and he'd be on a flat again, immersed in
the thick of the woods.

He loved flying through that stretch of leaves. There was
no need to time a damn thing. I know, you won't believe me.
Maybe he wasn't *that* good with the bike. The essential thing
wasn't to time the race though, but not to put his feet on the
ground during the climb, not to stop on the flat stretch to catch
his breath. That was his record.

As for the rest, from the point of view of our slightly
shorter and grungier Girardengo, if Adelaide were a sibyl or a
fairy, the fact that she lived in the forest meant something.

From the magnetic archive of Mr. Alex D. I'm
recording this cassette so that today's emotions don't
get lost like plumbs in the ocean.

I don't need a scooter, I don't need a motorcycle. I don't need to do my homework for tomorrow.
I don't need TV news, I don't need people, I don't
need a house. The cool breeze on my arms is enough.
The picture in my mind of Aidi sitting cross-legged

on her bed absorbed in her Greek book is enough. Her
class is covering the syllabus we did last year, Greek
lyrics and Oh my weary beloved and that Cecco Angio-
lieri dude. It's enough for me to know that in a few
seconds she'll hear my bike bell and come out to give
me a kiss. And when I throw it into the highest gear
and pedal those last fluid pumps going around the
seminary, then lock the wheel with the brakes and
fishtail into her yard, well, I'm convinced that heaven
is pretty much like this.

Adelaide is eating an apple. She's beautiful.
Her chestnut hair melts down her back. Her Jan-Sport
T-shirt makes contrasts against her dark skin, and
it doesn't manage to hide her reggae tits. I don't
know. It makes me feel weird. For the first time I'm
even looking at a girl's arms, her neck. It just makes
me feel weird. We hold hands and walk to the edge of
the meadow, then we sit next to each other. The hills
are lit by the warm afternoon light, the grass is
tender beneath us: everything is green and everything is good.

You've got this incredible look about you in
school, Alex, she says. Sometimes you look so pissed
off, other times it seems like your body is there
but your soul is who knows where. I mean, don't you
find yourself . . .

I started laughing and she put a blade of grass
in the crook of my elbow. And she's like, Why are you
laughing?

Jack Frusciante Has Left the Band

Because I'm happy, I think. That's what I told
her.

She laughed, then stuck her tongue out at me.

No, seriously, she says to me. Listen. At school
you always have that decadent poet attitude, but in
the afternoon though, you're mellow and sweet and . . .

I know. It's because *you're* here, my dear.

Another flash of the tongue. Half a kiss.

In those years old Alex was totally convinced that they needed to legalize drugs. Because if drugs were legal, the Mafia would be forced to flog those damn knock-off watches to keep afloat.

Meanwhile, in school, our political theoretician sailed through depressing D's and a stroke of half-assed luck here and there. A couple of teachers would've loved to kick him out along with all the other parochial punks, especially when the janitors found the newly repainted bathroom blossoming with autographed scribblings and subliminal messages like Beware of the rot-aryan skull, Alex is watching—that last brilliantly lucid message written in ten-inch letters with phosphorescent marker on the door inside the girls' room.

In a while Aidi was supposed to go to Prague on a trip with her class—alias all unknown twits absolutely unworthy of being mentioned.

They were already bustling with preparations. Indeed, a real twittering, full-of-shit rot-aryan, late-adolescent frenzy on the verge of nervous exhaustion just get the hell outta here already.

Old Alex wouldn't be going on the trip because his class couldn't find anyone to chaperone them, worthless up-to-no-good fuckups that they were.

Yo.

From the magnetic archive of Mr. Alex D. I hate teachers. Enough sermons, okay? Enough with the fucking sermons, sirs. Sermons are henceforth abolished. Finished. Stop.

Then one fine morning the Latin and Greek teacher brought an album of Catullus songs accompanied by guitar and flute, then preached a more than discouraging exaltation of Eternal Love. She got hold of a lab technician who came in with some sort of prewar Victrola, and she had him play the album. All those insipid declamations with flutes, static and popcorn in the background. An unbelievably sickly sweet syrup.

Thence, after having tasted the *whole* album, the teacher asked the students what they thought of the syrup. Seeing as how some of the assholes in class must have gleaned some portents of satisfaction and deep sympathy from the whole experience, wouldn't you know they requested, good God, a repeat performance? After another twenty minutes of putrefying sounds, when the needle should've already been raised from the vinyl and put into its place like death itself, the Evervirgins Morelli and Musiani asked if they could bring that magnificent putrefaction home with them to listen to it again in their living rooms and maybe, why not? make a few copies on tape to give as gifts to their friends, my God.

What the fuck.

Old Alex and Depression Tony gave each other a knowing look more explicit than a call to 900–LUVLINE, and right after the bell rang for the break, with the class already empty, they did what they had to do: Depression Tony ransacked Musiani's bag quick as a cougar, and a nanosecond afterwards, the record was behind a radiator in the hall. Then two hours of math and various Cartesian axes to intercept Entities equal to $x + z$ and still no look-see into the bag on the part of Musiani. So the twelve forty bell rang, and Alex and Depression Tony strategically prepared and catapulted themselves out of the class, already dressed and bags in hand.

Finally, a few minutes in the bathroom waiting for everyone to file out, and last but not least, shoot down to get the record. That selfsame afternoon, both of them equipped with wool gloves so as not to leave any fingerprints, while Depression Tony held the vinyl in the most propitious position, old Alex screeched a jigsaw through the album with the devotion of a Carthusian monk, and less than a half a minute later, the selection of Catullus songs was divided into two almost equal halves that yearned to be slipped into padded envelopes and brought to the Evervirgins Morelli and Musiani.

Well, what the fuck.

And while Aidi was hanging out in Prague there were the elections. Unfortunately old Alex couldn't vote, otherwise a whole slew of leftists would've gotten one more vote. I mean it's all right to be an anarchist and all, but when you're just about to vote and find that Christian-Democratic cross and shield or the Socialist carnation on the voting form, it just blinds you. And then it dawns on you that the family with glasses sitting in the seat behind you voted Social-Democrat-Christian straight down the line with a couple of geriatric friends of the family as their favorites; and so you gotta throw all your weight behind the opposition, no? I mean, what the fuck.

So the whole week before the election went by with Alex tearing down posters of the Party in Power and fleeing cougar-like on his bicycle.

Christ. It was *great*.

The antiabortionist Casini appeared live on TV, practically in tears, and old Alex felt so overwhelmed by the bombardment balls of joy, he was almost congratulating himself with a quick two-fingered wank right there on the spot.

Even if when all was said and done everything went back to the way it was, and the thieves kept stealing despite the hundred votes less in Benevento and Latina, well . . .

Well, you had to build a new Italy, because the first Republic was a total failure, and in the meantime Alex had become an anarchist waiting to join up with Durruti's bunch and their red and black flags. The next year he'd be eighteen himself, and then he'd fuck everyone at the elections.

He hadn't seen Martino since the week before his physics test, but he didn't miss him. Until one afternoon of blinding light Martino got around to calling him. It was a long and strange afternoon, which later, before he rewound this piece of his life and put it in a dark drawer, old Alex would remember as that fucked up Monday in April.

Martino was in the house alone, as always, talking on the phone, and from his usual "What's up, Alex?" you could tell for miles he was seriously bummed. Then, after a few unsuccessful attempts, pressed by Alex's questions, he let it out. Two weeks earlier Martino got pinched by the cops in Riccione, coming out of a disco, lit up to the gills and sick. In his pocket he had half a sheet of acid. He talked in a low voice, hoarse, with the stereo on in the back. He was already high and didn't want to know about what Alex was up to. Martino was desperate and didn't give a shit.

"Alex," he said in a low voice from the other end of the line. "Good God, Alex. I don't know if I can deal with it anymore, you hear what I'm saying? I hate *everybody,* you hear me? They're all so full of shit, my man. All they tell is *lies.*"

He said it like this.

". . . I was sick, and those assholes wanted to see my license . . . Get out of the car asshole, and show us your license! What's wrong with this jerk? What're you high on *jerk?* . . . They laughed at me, the assholes, and I told them to get their hands off me, the bastards, don't even think of touching me, and they got me good, they found the trips in my pocket and they held me against the car like a sack of shit and now come with us, asshole, we'll take a ride to the station, understand? you understand Italian, right? . . . What the fuck could I do with those pricks holding me down, and put your head down cuz everyone's looking at us, you see your friends? those are your friends, jerk, and y'know what they're looking at? they're looking at what happens when you go out all dosed up, ugly asshole . . .

"Asshole was all they knew how to say . . . They kept me there for a day . . . Alex, there's gonna be a trial now, you hear me? . . . And my old man, when he came to see me *pretended* to be pissed off, but inside he didn't budge. I know how he is. I know him, that bastard. He'll find me a lawyer and that's it. I was desperate, and he pretended to be pissed off, but inside he didn't feel a thing. Total zero, *nothing,* y'dig? He'll find me a *prestigious* lawyer, dig?

"They know everything in school, don't they?"

Martino wanted to know all of it.

And who knows how some of the parents were enjoying the fact that the bad apple got what was coming to him; because someone like him was unacceptable in school, and they wouldn't need exams to cut him down now, because the voices and parents' comments were enough—all the asshole-mothers-with-makeup-and-short-skirts' talk, because as long as you dose with their girls and fuck them discreetly while their parents are at dinner with the Lion's Club, everything's all right, no? But now they needed to protest and complain to the principal, lest it be known that Elsamaria and Selvaggia were in the same class with that degenerate, drugged-out pusher . . .

"I'm nobody to no one," Martino told him. "Yours truly is worthless. I thought I might've been something to a few girls, but not even that's true, because they're all sluts the ones I know, and one guy's as good as the next. They get themselves fucked, listen to Carboni, make you stupid, get fucked again, listen to more Carboni and make you stupid . . . And money, money, money . . . Just piss it away, all the money . . . I spend a million lire a night, Alex man . . . I disgust myself, y'dig? . . . I don't wanna be like this and I can't be anything else."

Alex would've liked to say, Just cool out, Martino, you'll see, we'll find a way out, you got a bicycle man, why don't we go for a ride together through the hills, it's sunny out, listen, and it's a lot less horrible if you find someone to cycle with, y'know bro? . . . He's never heard old Martino cry or talk like that; so desperate and angry that he kicked the stereo at one point; because along with the tears and the rage, Alex heard something crash on the other end of the line, and then the music stopped. A second later the telephone went out, and when Alex rushed to call him back, and then every time afterwards that he tried to get hold of him, there was nothing but a busy signal. Martino must've taken the phone off the hook, and the rest of the story was like it was already in the newspapers, in one way or another. Common knowledge.

What neither the journalists nor the police could've ever known was the letter that Martino had sent him after that phone conversation. One side of a sheet from a spiral ring notebook with small nervous letters written with a black Bic.

The only person Alex showed it to was Aidi. There are certain secrets that are too terrible for one person's conscience alone.

Alex, my buddy,
Once this letter is finished, I'll go down via dei Colli, via San Mamolo, via d'Azeglio and via Farini full speed on my famous Vespa Special, I'll stop at piazza Minghetti across from the post office, get this letter out, maybe get an ice cream (I could go for a tutti-frutti with cherries on top), I'll come back, leave my Vespa in the garden, close myself in the house and destroy all the paintings my folks bought for me to make this dead place beautiful.
Living like this disgusts me, and I'm too far into it to change.

All the same, my poor folks can't be blamed. It's not because of them that I made this decision. It's for me.

I thought about it and thought about it, old boy. These are my conclusions: if you're a bum, a druggie, a marginal, an Albanian, you're fucked. They isolate you and you're outside the group. Then the group leaves you more or less in peace and off to the side in the beginning, until you get too big, and then you wind up in prison.

If you're a normal person though, respectable, if you're in the group, for better or worse, you work for the group. And that doesn't necessarily mean being honest. In fact the heads of the groups are like my friends. With their political parties, their censorship, economic interests. You know loads about all this stuff being a sort of social outcast yourself.

And the group is all the shit they give us to eat, right? So there. I believe there's a way out though, that if you're superintelligent or spiritually liberated like a Buddhist monk or a great philosopher, you can rise above it; or you take your sleeping bag and go live in the train station or in the nomad camps, and then you go below it all. I can't go for the first solution. It's too hard. And then the only intellectual thing I've ever done is watch movies. I can't deal with the second one either because I'd get sick immediately. Being a bum I'd get all crusty and decrepit and ugly.

There's a third way though, in the end: a leap out of the circle they've drawn around us. I just get a little grossed out thinking of how my body will be. Last night I had a dream of the rescue squad coming into the house, busting the door open and finding my corpse.

I was lying on the floor belly-up. The paramedic was fat, around fifty, with a black mustache. He picked my head up and said: "Poor guy," like in the movies.

But I'm cool with myself, you know Alex? Because it's the first big thing I've ever done. All the rest is what they taught me. I was the one who planned and decided this gig.

Alex, believe me, I'm serene.

Good-bye and a big hug with all my might. Don't let the bastards bring you down. Don't forget me.

Martino

The letter was in a yellow padded envelope. Inside, together with the sheet of spiral ring notebook paper, there was a tape; and on the tape case there was a Doors line added: "It's the strangest life I've ever known." Alex knew that tape well, it was a Diaframma compilation that Alex had lent to Martino a couple of months before. LIBRA—SIDE B was written on the sticker.

He'd forgotten that cassette, almost buried it with the other summer compilations and stupid disco hits, but Martino listened to it and was struck by "Libra," the angriest and hardest-core song.

Alex waited until Sunday afternoon, when his folks went out, and then gave the tape a listen, turning the volume up full blast, the bass loud enough to damage the woofer, while Frederico Fiumani's asymmetrical voice went: "Dedicated . . . to punk . . . rock" with the buzz of a live recording in the background. The applause came right away, and the band kicked in and it was like Martino himself, roaring the first lines into the mike. Then the "Anarchy in the U.K." riffs, and the lyrics slamming over all of it, thrashing themselves to death with head butts in the face, and at a certain point our helluva guy felt his eyes very lucid and

"Thank you all, good night, ciao," Frederico Fiumani said at the end of the piece. Then even Alex wailed without opening his mouth, Hit the past in the heart! . . . Destroy the future! And in this dark drawer's story, Martino's funeral was in the afternoon, and there weren't more than twenty people there to bid the old boy farewell. From the hundreds of guys and girls he'd shared his life of acid and fast lanes with, only one beacon from the overtwenty-year-old crowd showed up, with Ray-Bans, blue jacket and Mercedes with Verona plates. But he seemed uneasy. He left before the end.

From the magnetic archive of Mr. Alex D. I
was the one who showed the newspaper article to the
parental units. I wanted to keep them from finding
out on their own and thinking there was something
fishy because I hid it from them. The photo published
by the local newspaper, though enlarged, was the same
as the one on his ID card, with the long sideburns
and that sort of smiley beach bum face.

The parental units hardly ever heard anything
about Martino, so they weren't that worried, but they
gave me the third degree all the same. They wanted
to know if I'd ever seen drugs around, in school, or
if I'd ever taken any. And I was like: No, no, no. I
swear. Tell us the truth, son. It's better to tell
the truth now than find yourself in a situation like
that poor boy. No, no, no, really, I'd tell you, I
swear. Promise? I promise, definitely.

In the end the Chancellor came to the conclusion that Martino must've been some sort of miser-
able wretch and that's it, a guy who happened to fall
in with a bad crowd of pushers and probably killed
himself because they gave him the choice of either
killing himself or getting killed by them. As he elabo-

rated out loud on his private-eye deductions con-
cerning the poor wretch in front of the family, all
nodding with assent, I swore to myself I'd never show
the letter to the parental units. Never. Because people
don't understand, and they don't even do it on purpose: they just don't get it.

The family always puts the old newspapers in a
bin which my brother empties out from time to time
in exchange for a little tip. But I made sure to
take the newspaper with Martino in it and throw it
away that same night, to keep my mother from reading it to my grandmother over the phone, or to keep
my brother from cutting out the article and showing
his friends.

They thought about it a lot in those first few days, sitting on the
sheaves of hay behind Aidi's house where no one could hear
them except for the wild boars and the neighbor's German shep-
herd. That's all he and Aidi talked about, and at times she would
cry, even if she'd never said a word to Martino. Naturally, at
school, all they talked about was old Martino. Alex, closed off
in the dark shell of his pain, knew that apart from three or four
people, no one seriously believed the bitter and fatalistic things
that were going around, and apart from those in his classes, the
other students hardly even knew him by sight . . .

"Aidi, every once in a while, I mean pretty often, not like
for hours at a time, but all of a sudden like, he comes to my mind.
And there's two things, you know? More than anything else,
that letter he sent me: it pops into my head in the most unex-

pected times and places, that letter . . . And then another thing, the one that cuts deeper . . . Even if we didn't hang out much together, him and me, during those days when we weren't in touch much . . . It's like, if I think he's dead, like he's not there anymore . . . If I think that besides everything, this guy doesn't exist anymore . . . I feel a huge pit in my chest, like a black hole that could suck everything up. It could happen, I mean sooner or later it will, to everyone, to my family . . . and then a piece of my life is gone . . . Like when my grandma dies, there'll be no one in that space of my life where I ate that soup with the star-shaped pasta, or when I felt my head burning and she put the thermometer in my mouth and covered me with that plaid blanket so I wouldn't be cold. I mean, when she dies all the relatives'll be around, the plants, the legal problems with the house, and all that will just bury my four-year-old curly-haired self with the blue sweater she knitted for me, my plate full of stars, and all those other times when I was a kid. Little by little, I'll forget them myself, I think.

"When my parents die I'll be grown up, shaving every day and shifting the gears in a car perfectly, but somewhere inside me I'll lose the time when my father took me to the zoo in Paris, and even that Sunday morning when my mother took me to the Cub Scouts for the first time and I was afraid we'd have to play dangerous games like jumping from trees, so I held my mother's hand real tight. Little by little everything'll go away, and maybe the only thing I'll remember is the hundred thousand times we fought—always the same, always more exhausting. Even my friends'll die, and meanwhile my lights'll go out too, little by little. In the end I'll die too and then it'll all be finished at that point . . . Maybe Martino thought likewise and decided to split the scene before everyone started dropping around him. Maybe he preferred to go away while everything was still whole . . ."

The first salt tears streamed down from tough-guy Alex's eyes, even if the tone of his voice was firm.

Then those two pirates hugged each other tight, without saying anything for at least fifteen blue, orange and green minutes. The tough girl we all knew Aidi was nearly felt like she was about to be buried at Spoon River.

Lots and lots of abbreviated afternoon study sessions, then off, *out,* pedaling away from the Matron's reproaches.

Millions of pedals, thousands of times getting to the seminary yard, thousands of cruises downhill on the unpaved road, thousands of skids à la Girardengo in front of Aidi's house, thousands of times under the sun, thousands of times the green grass and the scent of that deep vegetal world, thousands of times Aidi coming to open the door, leaving her notebooks open on the kitchen table, saying, I only have a little more to go but I'll finish it after dinner . . .

And maybe it doesn't seem like a big thing, those two pirates just chilling out on the bed, fully clothed, hugging each other tight without talking; or the idea of our strong silent type watching her get into playing the guitar; or them cutting their initials into potatoes, H and J, like Holden and old Jane, frying them, then eating them together. But those were the things that happened in those days. The quarter hours of May were dripping slow and dense, and Aidi and Alex sat on the veranda listening to Edie Brickell's "Hard Rain's A-Gonna Fall" and "Circle."

In the low-voltage year of their separation, Alex would remember the gravel crunching under his Doc Martens, his hand going across a vein of rust on her garden chair, the cold marble table where they set up the radio and sheets of paper and colored pencils.

And just when our helluva guy was drawing Aidi with one of those enormous smiles like the ones certain minor artists around seven or eight years old draw, or when he grazed her wrist, or kissed her slowly on the cheek, he knew in his heart of hearts that it couldn't get better than this.

The moment of departure was approaching, and the two of them had decided to spend the last few days together before saying good-bye.

After substantial negotiation with the family, old Alex's situation outlined itself more or less as follows: he'd leave Bologna in the middle of May—in any case you didn't get much done in those last days of school (not that during the rest of the year he broke his back, of course)—to go to England and study English. At the end of May, back to Italy. Then he'd spend a week at home with the parental units. His folks would split for the mountains and the tough guy would camp out at his grandmother's so he could share another week with Adelaide until she went to Sicily to say good-bye to her cousins and relatives before—here we go—the Big Trip.

One afternoon, while our helluva guy was ready to go home, Adelaide stuck a piece of paper in his hand. "Open it tonight, after dinner," it said. "When you're in bed with a nice cassette in the background." That night, after dinner, he lay out on the bed and whatnot with *Bob Marley and the Wailers Live* in the background. He unfolded the piece of paper from the pocket of his jeans and read.

> At home, before you get here.
> Alex,
> These days have been real weird. The more time passes, the more I feel my emotions growing, and even the fear of the Big Trip to America. It's real hard to describe. All I know is that I'm going to be totally alone, and it's the first big thing I've ever done. I decided it, I set it up. And now the big day is approaching. Meanwhile we spend loads of time together, and every day I feel more and more like I'm moving inside you. There are times when I feel like one person with you, and in other moments I feel far away, and I'm scared, but all in all it's incredible, this has never happened to me with anybody. Maybe we're still not able to totally understand all of it now. All I know is that it's good like this, and I hope June lives up to everything that happened before.
> I've already got the notebook ready, as soon as you get back from England we'll start to write.
> I like you too much. I live you, even if it sounds stupid.
> A big hug.
>
> > Aidi

"I live you" didn't sound all that stupid, and even kind of takes the breath away, and personally, okay, even I'm pretty frazzled. But the story is this, not something else.

We'll have to drum up all the courage we can, I know, I know.

Depression Tony was already somewhat of a veteran, old Alex had only watched it being done and never even held a can of spray paint in his hands. Nonetheless, the idea was his, and the project came to fruition that afternoon.

So after a funky burn-the-allowance-money dinner at the McDonald's on the corner of via Rizzoli and Ugo Bassi, they went through the maze of little streets between via d'Azeglio and piazza Cavour. They tested the spray cans on the walls of an Institute for the Blind—dogs till the end, one would say in retrospect. Depression Tony gave a briefing on technique. At around ten, he and Alex plunged themselves into the movie-house darkness of via Codivilla, surrounded by a muffled silence broken at times by the rare car cruising by up the hill.

Every once in a while someone came by to drop off his part-time girlfriend on the street and split without hassling anyone under the curtain of trees on the opposite side of the street. Deathly afraid of getting caught by the cops, Depression Tony and the other exalted one executed their gaudy graffiti—containing the simple invocation AIDI—with two-foot letters on a column at the entrance to the public gardens.

Thus bringing their artistic gesture to fulfillment, Alex and Depression Tony split the scene joking and howling, while in the two Benzes with Modena and Ferrara plates, the irreproachable fathers of families were joined in carnal knowledge, panting and howling, with their respective part-time girlfriends.

From a strictly technical point of view, the graffiti was nothing special. But the youthful artist, old Alex, was sure that the colors were nothing less than extraordinary.

She'd see it Monday.

So between one painterly self-congratulation and another, they came to the final one-liners of May, the final school interrogations, the last cyberpunk anecdotes to memorize and tell the friends at the beach, the last cans of beer with the usual gang.

In the end-of-year school photos, Alex came out with a memorable junkie look, dressed casually with a green and white horizontally striped Glasgow Celtic soccer shirt and a dubious hairdo—like I just woke up on the wrong side of the bed and couldn't find a comb but luckily my hair is pretty short. Well, the sight of that noble countenance caused somewhat of a stir with the mothers of the Evervirgins in his class. Different from them, indeed—as they said in those days. The mothers didn't hesitate to ask with ovarian squeaks if the owner of that noble visage had anything to do with the young straight-A student who used to attend Middle School with their daughters.

From the magnetic archive of Mr. Alex D. This is for the parents of all my kotex classmates who find it hard to recognize me in the class pictures and ask themselves if this bad-ass dude has anything to do with that boy who was such an upstanding student once upon a time.

For your listening pleasure I've selected the Rollins Band kicking full woofer on the central stereo.

Well, yessiree. That bad-ass dude is I, you bunch of bastards. The bad-ass dude and the boy who always kept quiet while drawing, then read a book by Richard Scarry and knew the names of birds such as the bittern, the toucan and the now extinct dodo by heart, are one and the same. I is he, damn straight. The one who went to Elementary School dressed in Tyrolean leather shorts with pockets in the shape of oak leaves and a place for a knife is me.

The bad-ass dude who if it wasn't for his folks would've been long gone in the middle of the street, though they might throw him out on his ass anyway, is still and always me. The one who listens to that music-that-isn't-music-it's-noise cranking feedback and distortion full blast so as not to hear the little voice of his conscience telling him you're nothing but a scumbag drunk like that other six-feet-under loser and you don't know how to compromise and if you don't bend you'll break is still and always me, shit.

Well, come and get me, why not?

Man, I almost forgot. All your daughters, madams, make me puke. Your daughters, madams, would like to be sniveling sluts, but no one would do them. Why? you will ask. Well, because they don't know how to

let loose in the slightest. And if they seem like
little nuns in single file, it's not out of prudish-
ness or purity or anything else, but out of gross
fear. Anyway go fuck yourselves, all of you, if possible. *Thank you kindly.*

    End of transmission.

Okay. The second to last week in May our tough guy belly-
flopped the oral physics exam with some totally asinine blunders
on uniform motion and on the passage from the International
System to the other and vice versa. He threw himself tigerlike
into a dissertation on centrifugal force. Trying to surpass the
banality of the washing machine drum example, he couldn't
manage to find anything better than that damn amusement-
park ride where you buckle yourself into those seats that spin
around that metal pole that works like a hub and has chains
dangling from it. And so, the faster that gypsy roustabout makes
the ride spin, the more the seats with all those idiots aboard go
parallel to the ground. Because of the effect of centrifugal force,
period.

He barely got a D minus, but his folks would never find out.

Sunday mornings old Alex got up early while his parents were enjoying their dreams of the righteous, mounted his black bike and took a spin around the hills of Bologna.

Immersed in that beatific solitude, he saw at most only a few other heroic cyclists with whom he deigned to exchange warm and energetic greetings.

He got enormous pleasure from climbing the hills on San Mamolo Roncrio and via dei Colli, flying through the curves of Paderno, riding against the wall of Cavaioni park, coasting down the hills of Casaglia, then gliding into via Saragozza, while the city was waking up.

He got back home when the parental units had just begun to yawn in each other's face.

It was on such an exaggeratedly blue Sunday morning that he came into the house all drenched and sore to pick up the newspaper and read that near Palermo they'd blown up fifty yards of highway to kill a judge who was the symbol of the war against the Mafia.

That was the Italy in which he was living.

But maybe it wasn't the Mafia. Maybe it was the Secret Service, or at least they had a hand in it—like in all the other terrorist attacks in the Republic—with the aim of diverting public attention from the Justice Department's investigations into corruption in the political and financial world going on in Milan, investigations which were getting ugly for the party bosses.

In short, this is the idea Alex got in his head: some government party representatives order the Secret Service, closely controlled, to create something particularly big—as big as the bomb in the Bologna train station or the one on Train 904—to show that the public was horrified and squarely behind the Democratic Institutions—institutions represented by the government party. All this in order to loosen the choke hold around their necks. So some more or less obscure director of the Secret Service decided that this brutal death sentence would've outraged the country and be blamed on the Mafia. Sort of a perfect plan. Whether the Secret Service would have to carry out the terrorist attack on their own or give the Mafia the means and protection needed to do it in order to eliminate enemy number one made little difference.

Old Alex went ahead with this line of thought, sitting in the living room with the newspaper open on his lap, remembering the terrorist attacks of his childhood. He'd heard the huge rumble of the Bologna train station when it was blown to smithereens; and then there were the ambulance sirens as they sped along via Porrettana toward the Apennines the night of the San Benedetto bombing; and then.

That was the Italy in which he was living.

So he stayed home all day, angry and caged in, convinced that the way it was in Italy, and in all the rest of the Grown-Up World, was a lot like it was in school. Brute strength and ignorance dominate; whether it's the Mafia boss with a gold chain around his neck and an Uzi in his drawer or the haughty teacher sneering at the students' political opinions, or the way they dress, or that government undersecretary scarfing down a plate of pasta with salmon in a Roman restaurant without ever paying his bill . . .

That afternoon old Alex saw Nanni Moretti's *Il Portaborse* again and came to the conclusion that a man like Cesare Botero wouldn't've flinched in ordering the execution of whomever to keep his seat in Parliament. And there were too many men like Cesare Botero in the government . . .

Even that assassinated judge was someone who tried to leave the group—Alex thought, all mad and cooped up—one who couldn't stand the power mongers imposing their will on everybody, one who walked waist deep upstream until the rapids got too strong and dragged him away. He left the band, for sure. And when it got too heavy for the band, they blew him to smithereens with his wife and his entourage . . .

The going was getting tough, and the next day his Latin and Greek teacher, moved by the event, hung a portrait of the murdered judge in class, under the crucifix, behind the department's back. An hour later, the chemistry teacher made his semitriumphant entry into the class, fixed his eyes on the portrait, looked at the students with an interrogative air about him and asked who the guy in the picture was.

A minute later he moved on to questions about the digestive system, stressing chewed food, chyme and chyle, seeing as how he was behind schedule, boys.

That was the Italy in which he was rotting.

* * *

The last afternoon before old Alex's departure for England was a helluva dark and gloomy one. It promised rain like one of those illustrated reading primers with a story called "A Summer Storm." Everything was electric gray, and Aidi and Alex were supposed to meet at the corner of via Codivilla and via San Mamolo.

He locked his bike with two chains to the post of a billboard with a white poster that had something to do with the City Hall, so he whipped out his marker. Before he finished transcribing the lyrics to "Sunny Side of the Street," Aidi joined him on her scooter.

Alex liked her a lot. He liked her cheeks, her fingers, the way she hugged him. After all their late-adolescent greetings, she suggested they go take a spin around the hills, and our run-of-mill tough guy accepted right away, all enthusiastic and ready to fly on the wings of his imagination. He rode on the back of the scooter, less than an inch from her green sweater. She put it on to make him happy—Alex knew it—because that marvelous sweater intimated Ireland, the Pogues and happiness. All stuff old Martino would no longer experience, he thought at one point as the scooter cruised through the streets. He'd never again feel a lump in his throat because tomorrow morning he was leaving for two weeks and wouldn't see that special girl; he'd never figure out how one person is really different from another; never again get butterflies in his stomach about having to make a certain phone call for the first time; never get all happy to hear the sound of a scooter when you think you recognize it even though you're just dreaming in your own bed one spring morning; he'd never have a goddam thing again, no girls you hope to go to bed with, no albums to buy, no riffs to play on the Fender Jaguar . . . Martino would never again cruise through the hills with a girl, two on a scooter. Alex was trying to get used to this feeling, and then

when they got to the end of the 16 line Aidi went up the hill leaning forward, and he felt like they were a single thing, his chest against her back and his hands on her hips. Her hair flowed out from her helmet, and a Smiths song came to Alex's mind, "There's a Light That Never Goes Out," from *The Queen Is Dead,* where he says something like "Don't take me home tonight because it's not my home, it's theirs, and I'm not welcome anymore. And if we get hit by a double-decker bus, it would be a pleasure and an honor to die by your side."

And that's nothing on tape. Alex saw an old concert on MTV, and for starters there was Morrissey with that triumphant jacket and open shirt, dancing like a clown, epic and grotesque at the same time, a bouquet of withered white flowers in his hand, a sublime allegory reminiscent of the Sex Pistols' "We're the Flowers in the Dustbin," and as soon as they kicked in with "and if a double-decker bus crashes," the theater explodes, and thousands of fans are singing in a chorus about *how much* they dream of dying together.

Well, that's just what came to his mind. Not that he hoped Aidi would shoot into the next curve and splatter them across the embankment. But the magic of being together did come back again, along with the charm of not knowing *exactly* what to do with each other because—ooh—just holding hands they had it all.

* * *

Finally they landed in a little unknown square, a sort of deserted parking lot surrounded by trees. An absolute peace ruled that place, and our pirates sat on a step—a situation where people sitting in normal chairs hardly look at each other—and then, in one of those way out of the book moments where they're looking into each other's eyes from six inches away and there's no script to read from, our tough guy threw out one of his nearly immortal lines: "Today, Anna, that girl in your class with blue eyes gave me an incredible letter. Like when she sees me she understands that I'm different from the others, and she knows what I'm thinking when I'm off doing my own thing, and would be real happy if I talked to her, and well, I think she wants it bad."

And then.

"You see. This coming year is already planned out from top to bottom. I'm already on Anna and Federica's agendas. With one I have to play the cerebral leftist into underground movies and philosophy books. With the other I can be a little more pop, almost glam, and have her introduce me to her parents and call her every afternoon at the same time. With one I have to laugh at my somewhat bestial friends—they're rowdy and whatnot because they don't have a clue, but deep down they're all right. With the other I have to give up all the piece-of-shit parochial punks—drunks, druggies and hooligans straight out of a sermon by Father Pius, who'll set you all straight and make you get that filthy disgusting hair cut by a *real* barber, a part of my past I'd forgotten. But the fact they expect these things from me isn't so bad. Everyone tries to manipulate others into their own personal theater. What's worse is that I do all the things expected of me, one move right after another, and act in their squalid or trivial or tragic little scenes and then laugh to myself. But I'll do anything they want, because the only way I can feel alive is to constantly change, always put on a damn act. Up to now I've had nothing but crap parts. This one's boyfriend, the kind teenager who helps a lady onto the train, or the urban grandson. But this is just off-off Broadway. Give me time to mature and I'll make it big playing the unsuspectable whitecollar whoremonger who whips his children with a belt, or the bald, entertaining and masturbatory math teacher . . ."

Maybe Aidi didn't understand it deep down. Or maybe she did. On the other hand, it was always a matter of devastatingly important ethno-philosophical questions, and therefore, I mean.

At one point he threw a playful fake punch at her, but he wanted to kiss her *seriously,* and then bite her a little and tie her to him and not let a single drop of time left together drip away . . .

"What are you going to do next year," Aidi said, "when you want me to be here?"

"Well, I think I'll write you. I'll sit at the windowsill with a heavy gray sweater and I'll be sad. Look, you don't really realize how important you are to me . . . Everything's changed since I met you. I mean, you know . . ."

"Alex, I feel bad when you talk like that, like you're not important to me, like you're the only one who's doing anything. I don't know . . . Sometimes you come out with these things . . . Look, you're real important to me."

"Yeah?"

"Sure. Why are you acting like this?"

"Come on, Aidi. I know I'm important to you. I just need to hear it over and over again. Look, it's beautiful. And don't think that even if I say it a lot it's less true, or that if . . ."

"I like you too much, Alex."

"Yeah."

(May through the hills. Cool breeze, clouds, cars passing every ten minutes and all the rest.)

"So when I get back from England and June comes, we'll do the notebook, deal?"

"Deal."

Then, our pirates sat together close as close can be until that predinner time came, around seven twenty. The next morning, our tough guy was at the airport escorted by the parental units, ticket and boarding pass in hand, when all of a sudden Aidi appears from nowhere. She came on the scooter to say good-bye. The Chancellor and Matron kept themselves discreetly off to the side. Alex was absolutely radiant, and when he got in line with the other passengers she even told him how cute he was. So that morning he took off all smiling with some commercial rock in his head—something like a disco remix of the Dead Kennedys' "Holidays in Cambodia"—full of concentric emotions because the rebound from England was in June, and then th-th-that's all, folks.

Two weeks in England and between worries about how to get the bus from Heathrow and the return trip to London he was embedded in the English course, the Benettonesque faces of

Paulos, Ivan, Shoko and all the other friends he made in front of the toasted chicken sandwiches in the school cafeteria; the cricket match on the stubbly grass with a less than spectacular outfield; snooker games; nights of darts and underage drinking at George's Inn; a couple of days varnished in a hangover; rude awakenings at six in the morning because the window didn't have blinds; sly coyote smiles at the blonde girl who came around with the newspapers; a couple of literally insignificant dates; some free concerts . . .

And in the end, even that big bass drum beating 2/4 in old Alex's chest.

Because now, folks, it was really *June*.

Third

The Chancellor called
Heathrow airport from Italy

The Chancellor called Heathrow airport from Italy and asked the Alitalia desk manager if it was definitely the last time flight AZ 1236 due to leave at 17:00 would be delayed.

The flight to Bologna was first bumped to 18:20, and then even to 20:40. Meanwhile the other airlines rolled onto the runways, scoffing at us on the way to their destinations, toward a thousand places with the same carpet and the same air-conditioning. Sure of themselves to the point of arrogance, the masters of the house ran the show. The giants of British Airways elbowed past Air France and Lufthansa, the new masters of Europe. It was worse than on the ski slopes in the Alps, where German kids all wrapped up in their fluorescent antiavalanche snowsuits had only to adjust their goggles in order to humiliate all the whiny snot-nosed shivering little Italians too stiff in the knees, falling back on their asses destined to slide into the snow crying for their mothers.

The Japanese tourists were amused to listen to the Mediterranean musicality of their Alitalia check-in call.

"I can't show up looking like this," someone must've said.

Alex slipped into the bathroom to change his sweaty Fruit of the Loom for a more than respectable apricot-colored polo shirt. He washed his face one-handed because he had to keep the button for the cold water pressed down with the other and combed his hair with his wet hand to get that fake gel look. He had a three-day beard, and his face was so tan that he could've passed for a college student, or at least a young man worthy of some respect, a goal from which the date on his passport and ID card separated him inexorably: barely seventeen and a half, no car, didn't smoke cigarillos, didn't know how to dress with taste . . . In a few words, old Alex felt he didn't have the attitude of someone with a house full of hip *Corto Maltese* comic strip posters, a steady but not too steady squeeze, some sort of job, decent parties to go to and a motorcycle, and.

He could imitate or trace all these God-given attributes, but he couldn't reproduce them *exactly*. He would've needed years. Meantime he'd have to learn how to recognize wines and get rid of those *humongous* basketball sneakers.

With some seventeen-year-old guys (the girls are another story, more complicated) you don't have to talk but ten minutes to figure out how damn insecure they are.

"Just listen to how we talk," the tough guy thought to himself. "We throw out all this acrobatic syntax and still can't be hip about breaking the grammar rules . . . Our slang always has something to do with our scholastico-masturbatory world. There's none of that jazz-head detachment I hope we'll manage to get with time . . ."

But after all that hesitation, our tough guy was almost sure: it was *only* a matter of time. And that straightedge understood from the way the woman working behind the counter flashed a fake smile at him that the world of civil aeronautics was an inferno of depravity, and the lives of stewards and stewardesses a tangle of unmentionable promiscuity.

All in all, she didn't give him that condescending look she used with kids, nor did she have that hassled expression they get when a ball-busting teenager straight out of *Encino Man* arrives. Christ, she was looking at him *professionally,* as if he were a respectable customer, a fucking respectable customer.

Then, talking to the desk manager on equal terms, that madman experienced an unknown shudder and the obscure feeling of being some sort of spy in enemy territory: "Sir" "I'm sure you'll understand" "We're having some minor technical problems."

An award-winning performance by Girardengo. A polished actor. And he managed all of it without shitting his pants from the excitement of finally being considered an adult, up on cult books like *Confessions of Felix Krull* and *The Cream Train.* Still, something in the center of his mind made him afraid that from one minute to the next the man in the jacket with fancy trim would get up from behind his desk, look him straight in the eyes and hiss at him an inch from his face: "You think we don't know what crap music you listen to? You think we don't know you got a pair of combat boots and a Sex Pistols T-shirt in your suitcase? That's not music, it's noise! Now beat it before I sic the dogs on you, you late-adolescent piece of shit!"

Well, the time of departure seemed definite now. At 20:40 the technical difficulties troubling the DC-9 would be a memory, the motors would roar—the plane would roll up to the runway, and the captain Pusceddu would raise all the Bolognese in flight with egg on their faces for having made such a bad impression in front of all the world's airlines. Still, in a trivial way they were happy to be going home. And old Alex would be able to strut out of that Alitalia cage all pasty with the satisfaction of having quite successfully gotten through one of the twenty-nine initiatory rites into adulthood.

Just under three hours to departure and the tough guy had nothing to do and would've rather done anything—dance to the rhythms of the lamest Pet Shop Boys album at a rave party, stay back to help the desk manager or scrub the floor—than just stay there twiddling his thumbs, which was too ludicrous a damnation to deal with.

So once again he assumed a less soldierly demeanor—dragging his feet and abandoning that solid North Italian manner—and shuffled off into the neon-lit newspaper stand cum stationery store cum candy shop.

Inside there were whole shelves full of M&M's triple the size of any he'd ever seen in Italy, shit. Laid out on the cover of the *Daily Mirror* in full color was a girl with two planetary tits covered by a semitransparent veil promising more on page 9. Some young guy with a purplish face couldn't keep himself from flipping through the pile of newspapers, hoping no one would suspect he was getting an eyeful of page 9.

Two rowdy girls from Rome, saggy asses, ogival hair, wearing ridiculous leggings with horizontal stripes, were exchanging full-mouthed chuckles and pats on the back. They couldn't decide whether or not to buy one of the magazines on the shelf with the various *Playboy*s and *Mayfair*s. The cover of the magazine had a muscular dude with the face of a faggot archangel smiling maliciously, flexing his biceps and tugging at his goods. The periodical seemed to tempt them irresistibly. The chicks wore identical pairs of black sunglasses and they were very embarrassed and couldn't decide and continued to giggle and that's all. Flushed with shame, they extended and retracted their arms at the totem which was the source of their squeaky secretions: "Pervert" and "No, you!" and "Why don't you get it!" All of a sudden Alex got a cinematic flash that made him giddy: one of the two girls, back in Italy, tells seven or eight of her identical friends, with denim jackets, leggings over bulbous knees, Stayfree pads and blue Keds, how much fun she had in England with Maddalena. "We met some really nice guys from Milan that might come and see us this summer and one of them's name is Simone, just tooo hot, I got a picture of him here and we got drunk almost every night!"

When the giddiness was over, old Alex split for the exit clutching a music magazine and a chocolate bar. Then, at eight, after the longest hours of his life were spent in the airport's Our Price Music Shop reading the song lyrics in cassette cases, he looked up at the departure screen and saw that the red light next to his flight had lit up, and this coaxed him toward the check-in. Anyway, the Red Hot Chili Peppers' first guitarist was one Hillel Slovak, presently dead, to whom they dedicated the *Mother's Milk* album, and that very morning Alex read in *Vox* that now Jack Frusciante had just left the band.

Jack Frusciante was the new guitarist and had been with the band for a couple of years. He was thin and muscular, around five foot four, real squat compared to the classic California beach hunks. Anyway, he had memorable hair, pre-Beatles bowl cut or shaved except for a tuft coming down over his eyes, and seemed to live in his skate jams and sneakers. He was always in the shadow of the other band members, since the Chili Peppers' stage was monopolized by the antics of Anthony, the vocalist, and the more than flamboyant Flea on the bass, who in the "Behind the Sun" video appeared in a pair of pants made out of toys—like dolls, blocks, plastic puppets and stuffed animals.

Old Frusciante wasn't an extraordinarily talented guitarist, but he did what he had to do. He grooved with the band's fluid electric sound without raising his eyes, without fixing in on the camera with a hallucinatory gaze like Flea did. Alex especially remembered him in the "Under the Bridge" video, where he played the intro on a Fender Jaguar, wearing a hooded Peruvian shirt in front of a tacky western backdrop. And now, for some unexplainable reason, old Jack Frusciante left the band. Now that they didn't have to play for a few bucks and free drinks at some Hollywood club or underground festival, now that they were raking in shovels full of dough and in the middle of a world tour. Now that they had a gold record, the Grammy Awards, fame and security, he just up and left.

And maybe on his own he would have been a nobody, because he was still too unknown. So it wasn't a question of making a move like Peter Gabriel leaving Genesis at the height of their popularity to go off on a more satisfying solo career.

For Jack there was probably only Hollywood, drugs and a new local club band to go back to; and the managers would've written J. Frusciante, former Red Hot Chili Peppers guitarist on the posters in fluorescent colors, and he would've played there while the crowd smoked without giving him too much notice, and maybe someone with a good memory would've asked himself why he'd made such a stupid move . . .

Sure, it was hard to figure out such a seemingly inconsequential choice, but old Alex liked to ponder the subtle threads of Destiny and continued to rack his brains until boarding time.

Then, once he was onboard, he rediscovered much to his disappointment the provincial mind-set that he'd put on the shelf during that English parenthetical: the broad accents of his fellow passengers, the incompetence of the music editors in the Bologna newspaper—have you ever read the album reviews? or the movie reviews?—and behind him there was an absolutely soothing couple . . .

She seemed more of a twat than a pollyanna and was flying for the first time. She did nothing but quiz her boyfriend with Stupid Questions: Why are the wheels rising (dropping)? Where are the brakes? What city are we flying over?

He, on the other hand, seemed to possess a more complex personality. Besides qualifying as multitalented master of ceremonies with a couple of atrocious jokes about airplane disasters—two little anecdotes that nonetheless inspired a whinny of hilarity from his partner—he also took it upon himself to give satisfactory responses to her aeronautics quiz with very simple words, like It looks like we're standing still, but actually we're going very fast. He also peppered his answers with a few technical terms, a self-congratulatory effort right out of night school. The captain is dropping the undercarriage to create wind resistance. We're now flying over French (Swiss) airspace.

Alex fell asleep right before she asked, But what would happen if the window broke? He dreamed he was lying out on the edge of a huge pool with beautiful girls and his boyscout buddies and the gang from school and the punk catechist guitarists, even the ones he'd only seen occasionally and never exchanged more than two words with, or the ones who he hadn't hung out with in years, and everyone was mostly quiet, kissing all the girls, listening to Nirvana stoned off their faces on hash and Corvo wine and no one was puking or had to go back home before eleven or said that this wasn't music, it was noise.

When he woke up he flipped through the newspaper: the most interesting news was about a panther that had escaped from a circus and was wandering ferociously through the countryside of Central Italy. It's enough to say that this kind of news inevitably marks the Italian summers and leaves all the mammas breathless, and then they forbid their babies to go out and play in the garden for fear of seeing them kidnapped by a panther (I mean get real). This way they help lower the quality of Italian soccer. "Another two or three generations of panthers," Alex thought, "and we won't even win a UEFA cup."

The last English day was spent at the host family's poolside wearing down-to-the-knees skate jams. The newspaper headlines read "Heatwave" like in *Do the Right Thing,* and for that part of the world it was *seriously* hot.

In any case, Alex chilled out for nearly ten hours listening to the Pixies and the Pogues on his overheated Walkman with a bar of chocolate melting next to his head. Fact is he was developing a funky color now. Beige with fuchsia stripes.

Then, from the airport to the house, he got everything he'd expected: the Chancellor picked him up, then tortellini, some carpaccio with a lot of lemon, apple pie, and all the how did it go come on come on tell us and so on and so forth, until the tough guy once again took possession of his same old room: pictures of Malcolm X and the Sex Pistols over the bed, vegging out in a gray tank top and jeans, a bunch of letters from Aidi in the drawer, the stinky Nikes out on the terrace, posters of the Blues Brothers, Madness and the Clash, and an Orange demo.

From the magnetic archive of Mr. Alex D. Socialismo o Muerte. Got back today from merry old England, and the thoughts are boiling over in my head here alone in my room. The question that's been gnawing at me these past two weeks—maybe it's a step ahead or maybe it's just the basic premise of my theory on the Total Comedy: what sense is there in being sincere in life?

I mean, isn't it just a simple waste of time and nothing else?

Sometimes I think it doesn't pay to keep an upfront relationship with people—I mean with certain people, the ones that aren't worth going beyond any ready-made small talk or the mere exhibitionism of their own personal problems and all that coprophagous Is Everything All Right at Home? Better off acting

and cheating, no? *Everyone* plays the cynic, but the
real cynics are the ones that never confess it, the
girls that show off how they don't show off, the dawn-
faced ones who go to sleep at night and rise with the
sun and get over on anyone who wants to look at them
with the idea that they've finally found the right
girl, simple and true, even though she's only pre-
tending to blush.

If I were better-looking I could act in the
movies.

The truth is that my pact with the devil won't
let me do it. I just can't deal with the Dorian Gray
trip. I'm too unpolished, too imperfect. The character that most reminds me of the evil one's emissary
come to propose a Faustian pact was the postman with
strictly lateral hair that appears every other day
to make me sign for packages in the parental units'
absence or bring me postcards from friends raving it
up at some seaside resort.

But why this endless depression?

And most of all: why don't people have any style?

Gangsters wear sweatsuits and jeans, I'll let
you take it from there · · ·

Among the guys my age, Martino was far and away
the one with the most style. It's not enough to lie,
swindle and put on an act. You gotta do it well, for
free, with no ulterior motives. You gotta do it for
the love of the art.

Anyone would marry a rich woman to get money.
It's too stupid; ditto for buying a nice car to get
girls with, or staying with a chick only to have sex
in a closed room. These things are just bafflingly
plain.

Anyhow.

Am I ready to put my conscience and counter-
conscience underfoot and look for the things that
really make me happy, that make me feel good, make
me laugh and feel alive, seriously?

Yes, I'm ready. And that's not all. The point is
that I'm perfecting myself, because this is a difficult
matter. And I don't want to make the totally banal
mistake of negating existence or the fundamental
importance of feelings, mistakes that lead to squalid
late-life turnarounds, when you have to look for love
under the heading of the personals, payment possible
by Amex, Visa/MC or money order.

When you become a serious and dynamic fifty-
something professional with a lust for life and have
to look for a twenty-five max SWF wants serious relationship with mercenary loafer no drugs please, feelings begin to add up to about nine thousand lire every
twenty-five words.

Okay. I think I'm a thousand miles from any boring
disco hedonism.

It's all in having the right dose of feelings
and style. It's all in how you put together the

impromptu rage of punk and the most rigorous jazz rudiments to start the greatest revolt of all time.

Adelaide would never understand. No one would understand, but I'd like to sing it to her until she really gets into my world. If I were self-assured, I wouldn't be scared of America, or the future, or death.

Am I definitely crazy? Am I at the start of a road going nowhere? Am I at the start of a road going up? Am I in the band? Am I out of the band? Am I in the book? Am I out of the book? Am I in love with Aidi?

Would I be happy with her if she didn t leave for America, or is all that's happening just the head-rush of having so few days left together? Will we ever be together, like, Do you want to stay with me? Oh, yes dear! Would it be more beautiful than this? I don't know, I don't think so. The fact is every-thing's so confusing . . . Sure, I still don't under-stand why we don't make out and all. She's weird, that Adelaide who I didn't even know four months ago and now, well, now she's leaving me . . .

Well. Good night.

Be prepared, for you know not the day nor the hour.

He slept till late.

From the magnetic archive of Mr. Alex D. Need
to update the end of the school year. Went to the
gray Liceo Caimani to find out my grades, not to
mention what my friends got.

Tony double-flunked: Latin and Greek; Oscar and
I both paid for our granitelike indifference with
yet another professorial dis: they dropped us from a
C to a D in a spiteful gesture that stirred up all
our yawns.

I can just see them, all the teachers sitting in
a circle, with their asses and thighs suffocating
under skintight leggings making them sweat horribly.
They wear gigantic underwear. Reinforced, riveted,
armored. And Band-Aids on their ankles lacerated by
those old lady shoes they wear even in the summer.

They pontificate about the students' better or
worse intentions. I see Ms. Ciuncoli like in a picture,
with that horrifying summer suit, deciding who to
help or not. She stabilizes, cuts, synthesizes and
vents her frustration at never having been considered

by a man and having been chased out of the university: she still has her doctoral thesis deadline before
her eyes, the unattained tenure, the rigmarole of
all the exams, the honors course finished before it
started, the relegation to lower education . . .

This is my easy little world, Liceo Caimani in
Bologna, where I get involved in more or less friendly
relationships, buy snacks and keep my social skills
honed. This is the chicken coop where they teach me
to integrate with my peers. To stay in the group and
not raise my head.

And then there's Aidi, for whom no song or defi-
nition is enough, upon whom I hope God won't make it
rain. For our first date after two weeks of nights
throwing darts at George's Inn and coyote smiles
flashed at the blonde girl selling newspapers, we
agreed over the telephone to see each other in the
park, because it's really June, and this is the Here
and Now, and in two weeks we won't see each other
again, and.

(He wanted to hug her for a whole day straight, for all the times
he'd want to hug her and she'd be a hundred thousand miles
away.)

They went and laid out in the sun by the pond full of ducklings,
the same ones for which he acted out a hundred times the scene
of the ducks in Central Park when Holden Caulfield talks to

the cabdriver and asks him where the ducks go during the winter.

So there were all those marvels to rediscover, the sun, the ducks, the unforgettable novels. And then at one point, wouldn't you know it, the Mattia story comes out.

Christ, the scumbag was on her ass for the whole two weeks that Alex was away, and in a couple of words, he more than tried, shit.

The scumbag tried to come between him and Aidi.

In any case, Aidi gave him the preformulated "You're cute, and nice and interesting and all, but I don't feel like going steady with you."

My God, Alex had *nothing* against guys chasing her, nor did he have any right to complain, seeing as how they weren't even together, but the story with Mattia shook him up.

If he had come back from his fifteen days and nights throwing darts in London and Aidi had gotten happily together with some dude, Alex wouldn't've wanted to stay in Bologna; he would've immediately split for the mountains with his family after saying good-bye to her.

As for Mattia, he was an unquestionable son of a bitch. He never even gave a sign that he was interested in Adelaide and waited like a slimeball for Alex to be out of the picture before he pulled his shit. He's still a fucking bastard even if he already got his punishment.

(Alex's first instinct was to slice him up while laughing in his face.)

* * *

(In the end he realized it wasn't worth the trouble.)

He would meet him in the afternoon to explain the situation to him and invite him to stay out of the way until Aidi left. In the future they could still do things together, drink beer, steal records, go to parties, but as far as he was concerned the friendship was over.

Even if nothing changed on the surface, Mattia would still be hurt.

He was in the park, on foot, in the early-afternoon sun, standing before our protagonist. Mattia, sitting with his light blue long-sleeved Lacoste, had that tone of voice deserving of comprehension and spoke as if he were alone, justifying himself without Alex even asking. A far-off voice with a plaintive tone: ". . . And sincerely, I wasn't thinking of you those days . . . There's no excuse, look, because I know it wouldn't make any sense . . ."

The life of the park continued as usual: under the stunts of aspiring skaters, clumsy twelve-year-olds cruising along the black stripe of the road; grandmas walking children by the hand; a couple rolled in the grass like a hermaphrodite tumbleweed and the male part guided the female part's hand resolutely to his crotch.

He continueth speaking as one of the righteous.

(The author begs all possible pardons from those who may find themselves in the characters, or those who may have been explicitly quoted without recognizing themselves in any role. That is, except for Mattia. No pardon is begged from him. Be that as it may, this is the author's truth, and if someone hadn't told it he would've suffocated to death.)

He could've taken him by surprise with a combat boot in the mouth.

No, no, no.

Not because he was afraid though. He felt sorry for Mattia, that's all.

In the end, you don't put chicken thieves in prison.

He looked at him like Lee Van Cleef in the poster of *The Good the Bad and the Ugly,* and all he said was: "You know nothing. *Nothing.* You shouldn't have given a shit about *what* was between Aidi and me. You knew you'd piss me off by getting in the middle of it, and you did it anyway. You're miles from us, you understand? Now get your ass away from us. Go to the lakes in the mountains, go wherever you want, but don't try to see Adelaide again. Don't even call her. And don't dare dream about her, is that *clear*?"

Mattia was expecting Alex to be furious, and found he was remarkably cold and distant. In the end he shuffled away pretty quickly, walking off diagonally.

Alex caught up to him on his bike just outside the park: "I'm not someone who goes around threatening people, but I didn't do anything to you and you tried to fuck me. You broke the peace. I'm not gonna do anything to you because you've already been fucked up the ass, and I don't need any hassles right now. Someone else in my shoes would've waited for you by your house with two buddies. I'll just put you on probation. Think whatever you want, but the next time you get such a brilliant idea you'll have to pay for it. Right here."

As Mattia faded into the background, moving further away from his friendship, checking his back now and then, our tough guy threw himself into the road with the refrain from a Snap song in his head, and when he stopped at the traffic light he threw some punches in the air, thinking about Robert De Niro in *Raging Bull*.

Then he went to Aidi's house making odds on whether Mattia would call within a couple of hours. She said they shouldn't ruin their June because of some capricious little boy.

Well, that's right.

Eating cherries in the garden, Aidi pulled out what would become *the* notebook—a nice-looking Czech notepad—and then they finished by discussing the extent to which their relationship was exclusive. Thus they agreed not to talk about it anymore and to always do only what they felt like doing. If they trusted each other, they couldn't get hurt. Or maybe they could get hurt, real hurt, but it was June and they needed to live, not to discuss theory.

"Who knows if one day I'll be able to sleep at her place."

He knew well that none of the parental units would've ever allowed it, but he'd try to come up with something for next week, when the Chancellor and the Matron and *Frère de lait* were gone.

Lots of plans to take care of, things to do.

A big hug in the orange sunset, and he threw himself down the via Codivilla hill at top speed, enough mphs so as not to be able to open his eyes without having them tear up. His shirt adhered perfectly to his chest; his hair, appendices absolutely inessential for the moment's tension, were slapped back; his irregular nose cut the air that warned him of its palpable consistency, the pressure on his cheeks; triceps and back tensed. Do not impose any input onto his body other than to photograph it in an eternity of fifteen seconds. Without the muscles of his neck moving, his stare turned to the left for a hundredth of a second, as much as was needed to make sure no one had erased the graffiti, a flash of blue-yellow-green like a Newton album, schizzing out from the wall and smashing into the ceiling, and then the descent leveled off, the slope became more manageable, his sweaty locks stuck back to his head, the shirt became less adherent.

(Girardengo coasted to the point where he'd have to squeeze the brakes, but not too much if he didn't want to skid.)

(Via San Mamolo was one of those streets that seemed like an indisputable climb going up, but one that became just another flat stretch on the way back: you still had to pedal if you wanted to pass the row of cars stopped at the red light ready to dart into the little streets.)

From the magnetic archive of Mr. Alex D.
Evening. Sitting in a lounge chair on my terrace. It's chilly.

147

Listening to the Smiths on my Walkman while the rest of the family keep themselves company in the living room. I feel good.

Yesterday morning I was in London and now it's June and tomorrow there's only Aidi, even if I realize that while for me it's only one person leaving for Pennsylvania to stay for a year, she's got to say good-bye to a whole bunch of people, and sure, I'm a special person, but if I were in her shoes I'd want to do a whole bunch of things and hug a whole bunch of people. So I don't think I should hold it against her if she can't spend twenty-four hours a day with me.

All right. It won't be twenty-four hours. It'll be a nice morning and a quick afternoon date, just enough time to write something in the notebook.

Aidi wants to fill her eyes with people and places she won't see for twelve months, and I don't want to squeeze her too tight.

Good night everyone, I'm gonna go brush my teeth and put on a pair of shorts and go under the sheets with my Walkman on.

Bigmouth strikes again.

Nine thirty in the usual spot, between via San Mamolo and via Codivilla; chain the bike up to the billboard which now has all of "Sunny Side of the Street" written on it, hop in the saddle with

Aidi, and up into the hills, just like the day before leaving for England.

She wasn't distracted by Alex's stupid stories as he held her tight, wanting her to stop so he could kiss her, then take off again without saying anything.

"Alex, do you remember when you sent me that letter with the story of the little prince and the fox?"

"Sure."

"I really liked it a lot."

"I know."

"Yeah?"

"You told me so."

"Listen, I was thinking yesterday. Without this taking away from anyone's freedom, without this blocking anything, I think this situation has made us tame. We're starting to worry if the other's late . . . I'm happy when I see you, or when I'm with you. We've got so much to say to the other, and so much not to say, just staying together, quiet, next to the other and that's it."

(They were still hugging, even when the storm's first drops fell.)

Aidi would throw a party, a party for her departure. A good-bye party, or a going-away party. All in all, it was a party for her departure. There.

In the afternoon he took his guitar and went to Depression Tony's house in Ponticella. They jammed together, mostly blues rock using kitchen utensils for percussion.

They talked about various unimportant chicks that went out with this one and that one, strutting their stuff every which way. Then they listened to a demo of New Hyronia with Claudio Severi.

The morning of the party it was drizzling, and there was the well-grounded fear that they'd have to postpone the party because it was supposed to be outdoors with a bonfire and what-not. The people invited were mostly from her class, plus three or four friends she'd gone to Prague with.

Old Alex called her to be sure about what time to come over. Aidi's mother answered and she passed him on to her daughter.

"At five. Elena's coming too. That girl in your class I told you about," she said over the phone.

She had, in fact, mentioned her before. Very enthusiastically. Alex tried to picture her in his mind, but the image lacked contours. Anyhow, okay, he'd head up to Aidi's at five to give her a hand with the preparations.

The guests would arrive after seven thirty. Everything real laid back.

He wore a new meadow green Lacoste and white pants, hand-me-downs from Hoge. It was a real hit. He tried them on and they were perfect on him.

Alex seemed dead.

Sitting on the living room couch right after lunch, listening to the Clash turned up to where he couldn't even hear his neighbors having a row, eyes rambling, can of Coke on the floor, shorts torn in the crotch under a hooligan T-shirt. He gazed at the ceiling and worried about how many grooves separated him from the end of Side A.

In the end, *London Calling* should've inspired the movement of a few muscles whereby he could raise himself upright and flip the album over.

All of a sudden a woman entered the room. An *angry* woman. She spoke with a very high-pitched voice, like a young man, You cannot always stay here and listen to that music-that-isn't-music-it's noise, with the cold Coca-Cola on the floor and it's not even snack time and then you're belching all day long, and it wouldn't be a crime if you thought about studying once in a blue moon since you play the student but you're at the age where you should be working, and we can't put up with your moping around, young man, because now it seems you only have time for your friend Adelaide and you don't care in the least for your own family, but when you need something you surely don't go to the girls, you come to us, right? so try to show a little more respect, all right?

* * *

151

At five he got to the yard, panting in front of Aidi's house.

That he was listening to his Walkman while riding was more unique than rare. *Raw Power—Live in Parma.*

Kiss. Kiss.

"It looks like we're getting a little formal."

"Already."

He knocked the backs of her knees with his own and brought her to the ground, licking her neck while they laughed.

A pair of baking pans were on the table full of desserts still in an embryonic stage, surrounded by flour, chocolate powder, four or five quiches and an assortment of kitchen utensils. Our two pirates talked about Aristotle and Plotinus as they stirred the mixture with their spoons, careful to keep any lumps from forming in the chocolate.

Someone at the door.

It had to be Elena.

"Hi, how are you, Aidi's told me a lot about you."

"Yeah?"

Sure enough it was Elena.

She came across as a pretty acceptable character, a little conceited maybe. She was up on the study vacation in England scene and had a nihilistic look about her and she didn't seem like such a twit. Our tough guy gave her the old once-over out of the corner of his eye as he stirred the mixture of what was supposed to become some sort of zucchini casserole.

It was the first time they'd found themselves in that magic house with someone besides Aidi and her family. The mother, kind and generous, showed up with suggestions for possible snacks; Federico with his pistol and blocks; Aidi's dad, who would pop into her life once in a while, was looking more and more like some private dick from an American movie; Chiara, her older sister was sweet and beautiful. She really cared a lot about Adelaide. And then in a few hours the people would show up in throngs, and the atmosphere would become just a little more profane in that house surrounded by woods . . .

There was no need to freak out though. "The essential is invisible to the eye," said the fox. The people about to arrive shortly would eat, joke, kiss each other, tell stories, and then they'd go away and forget it all, without taking any of that magic place with them. They'd come in cars or on scooters, roaring up to the yard, and wouldn't understand a thing about how it feels to pedal up that hill, in the wind or under the sun, with the sparrows around them. Once Alex saw a squirrel, but it took off before he could convince it to jump into his arms to be taken to Aidi. For the others it would be nothing more than a dark, lamplit road.

From the magnetic archive of Mr. Alex D. Aidi's mother is really something else. With three kids so spread out in age, she's easily the busiest person I know—always kind, mellow and full of organic fruit and whole-wheat pasta.

After eight, the sun began to set. Francesca arrived, and her father said good-bye to Adelaide because he wouldn't see her for a whole year, and Fran would have to find a ride home, because we can't only live for the kids, and our plans, Mother's and mine, might just change tonight. He wouldn't see his daughter's best friend for a whole year and he said good-bye with the stupidest one-liner Alex had ever heard: "What're you gonna do over there in America? This is America. We've got our own America here!"

(Smash his face, throw him into his tin-can Fiat and bombard it with rocks while the asshole takes off down the hill with a mouth full of blood.)

He was the only one who didn't realize how sad and stupid the joke was, and he climbed into his car laughing and smiling all satisfied as he turned the ignition. He was going to go watch a good quiz show on channel 5, or maybe read a few pages of his best-seller before rinsing his mouth with Scope and shutting off the light. Maybe he'd pick up some ice cream on the ride home to surprise his wife. *Shit.*

Five hours later, even Pietro Rossi was getting ready to leave. He'd spent the whole party asking if someone could give him a lift home.

Then Alex helped Aidi clean up. It was a fairly cool party. Only he was wearing a Lacoste shirt and he'd probably catch a cold on the way home.

They wound up in her room, holding hands. She took a couple of pictures of him in black and white, then one of them together with the automatic shutter, sitting cheek to cheek under the *Gone with the Wind* poster.

Then she lent him a nice sweater with blue and violet horizontal stripes. See you Aidi, good night, see you Alex, tomorrow at three. I really like you, Alex. I like you too much.

Then the climb uphill, opposite from where the guests had faded away, along the secret path that went behind the seminary. The poor schmucks inside were all asleep. Aidi once told him that when she was ten or twelve, while she was playing in the park, a gang of seminarians saw her and yelled out "A girl! A girl!" and followed her for miles.

Back in the saddle. Yes, he had the keys to the house. Cool. Away on an emotional descent. Aidi was probably brushing her teeth. First he picked up speed on the flat stretch, then with a flick of the thumb let the gears jump against the back tire. A bit wicked at night, but otherwise he might've killed himself flying into the woods. First curve to the left. There, the slope was beginning. They spent a whole afternoon in April talking about if one of them got together with someone else. Alex was totally against it, and also a big hypocrite, since in London he'd been with some Polish girl for nearly *two hours,* and then even a Japanese girl, but he didn't know if that counted since they'd gotten together at George's Inn after four or five pints—it was the last night and all the Japanese and Arabs were treating big time—and he only realized what was going on once he had his tongue in her mouth, a perfect stranger with triple-malt breath leaning against a bench. Some Turkish guy passed by and said, "Good goin' stiff dick," in Italian and patted him on the back, giving him a sign that he'd buy him another round, but Alex declined, muttering, "Italy

Turkey, one face one race" because another drop of alcohol and he would've passed out in the Jap's mouth.

He saw her the next day before she was about to leave for Tokyo, and he couldn't remember what'd happened.

Yeah sure, but even if he had engaged in some extracurricular activity, he never diverted his attention from Aidi. And still he was afraid that if she got together with someone else he'd wind up acting out some obnoxious and sorry part, even if at that point he'd be the first to understand there was no more room for it. No tears, no talk. If Aidi got together with someone it would be so lightning quick he wouldn't even understand

and would split in silence, pedaling full force down the hill from the seminary, and in the next days he'd cruise the downtown streets alone, with an attitude on his face and his hands in his pockets, like De Niro in the *Taxi Driver* poster. Because our tough guy felt a lot like De Niro in *Taxi Driver:* a useless hero.

But it wouldn't really have finished like that, because Aidi wasn't the type to have affairs easily, and unlike him, when she did something she wanted to do it for real: he saw her dash out into the blue sky two thousand miles away and understood that whatever happens she'll always be inside him.

Straightaway at about thirty miles an hour. He could barely see twenty yards ahead of him with that ridiculous headlight. Fortunately he knew the road with his eyes closed.

Time to play a little chicken now.

Close my eyes? Close my eyes? Close my eyes?

One-two-three. Did it.

Turn to the left.

Next, a hairpin turn to the right.

He needed to brake a little or he would fly into the guard-rail. Sure, that's where the Orthopedic Offices were, and the receptionists would've have found him first in line, but still, he had to brake. Okay, everything under control, even if he did leave a little rubber on the asphalt, and then, further down, a straightaway, then a right, then a hairpin turn to the left, now the final stretch, another hairpin turn to the left, past the giant flower bed with fir trees and get to the automatic switch that opens the gate with two lions in front of it. Wow, that curve was right out of a motocross rally. He had to move to the left to get enough space so as not to hit the car parked in front of the watchman's house. The gate opened, via Codivilla at one hundred an hour, and back to sea level.

(He woke up all of via Saragozza screaming a caricatured throat-searing version of "White Riot.")

"Alex, do you ever think about how our story is totally crazy and doesn't fit into any picture, and how nobody understands it and nobody could ever understand it?"

"I think about it practically every day. I even wonder how much I understand it myself."

"A lot of people ask me why we aren't together and . . . I don't know, it's strange when you think about it. I guess if you look at it from outside we must look like two people who are together."

"I'm not with you because . . . because I'm cool with you like this, because June is fantastic, and knowing America's coming up on us we gotta say everything to each other because in a week it'll be too late. I mean it's awesome. I miss something though, and you know what it is. I'd like to kiss you and all the rest, but not just to do it . . . Really. It's hard . . . It's like setting you up to tame you a little more. It'd be harder to forget me that way. Let's get more attached with everything we do. I'm afraid of next year. I'll kiss a hundred girls, go to bed with people I don't even care about, but it won't be like going out with you and not saying anything for the whole afternoon. I already know that next year I'll do the easiest and most trivial things. With you everything's so see-through and childlike . . . If I think that I've never kissed you, Aidi . . ."

"You know that you always have to do What You Feel."

"Sure," I said. "I said What I Feel."

"And you still feel it?"

"I feel like this June I've been learning something new about myself every day, and with each new piece of me I discover another new piece of you, and every piece of myself I give to you I find one you left me in the stocking over the fireplace while I was sleeping, and it's beautiful. This has never happened to me. To see Alex and Aidi growing each day, every sunny morning that doesn't mean anything special to other people, and to go against the odds, and to laugh at the Oddsmaker, the one that was sure Denmark would've given up a truck full of goals and gotten eliminated in the qualifying rounds. But instead they did qualify, and they're playing in the European Cup with a real strong team, and the Oddsmaker can't make heads or tails of it.

People only understand once it's over, never while it's happening. Same for both of us. People don't understand how it's possible, seeing as how the Poll Taker categorically refused to believe that two people like us could have such a crazy story together."

"Fantastic. And how does Denmark play?"

"Good. You can tell they have fun."

"Alex," she said to him, holding his hand with a strange intensity that disturbed him. "I want Denmark to win."

From the magnetic archive of Mr. Alex D.
Reading Kerouac, and don't bust my balls for reading Kerouac, and listening to my records, and reading Tondelli and Andrea De Carlo, who are becoming my two favorite Italian writers.

I'm not really into seeing anybody.

I'm at my grandma's, preparing for the move with my Jollinvicta backpack full of books for appearances' sake, thrillers by local hacks, a pair of pajamas and two or three T-shirts.

Aidi's never seen my house.

In the beginning, when we first got to know each other, we arranged to come over to my place, but when I announced it to the Chancellor he got his bowels in an uproar. The problem was basically that she was a girl.

. . . Seeing as how you've got to earn your own space in this life, and how food always waiting for you on the table only makes you spoiled, which is the last thing you need, the least you could do is what some English students do and take the door off the hinges when they invite a girl to their room.

Picturesque, but what's the point?

It's a form of respect.

I mean really. Seeing as how I didn't want to put Aidi on display for the whole afternoon, I told her what the deal was and split, and so she's never been to my house.

So my folks are going away the day after tomorrow— their road trips are characterized by departures at ungodly hours like quarter to six. Of course, because you're all so *slow!* The house is to be locked and hermetically sealed, and if you're in you're in, if you're out you're out.

And seeing as how I wanted Aidi to see my house before she left, and my farsighted folks made me leave my set of keys with them so I couldn't go into the house, I made sure to get two duplicate sets made at the hardware store when I came back from England, just in case.

After tomorrow, by the dawn's early light, we shall use them to penetrate the mysteries of the occluded apartment, and should the phone ring I'm not to be disturbed. I'm reading *On the Road.*

The rendezvous is at three and I've got a sad taste in my mouth, because in the end I'm just so happy with Aidi, and when she leaves what'll happen? The punk-jazz revolution will start, and I won't believe in nothing and nobody no more and just live it up in the moment. That's the greatest thing Aidi ever taught me, even if she has a different take on it and is so sweet and naive and trusts everyone, even the first Mattia guy that gets on her ass. She thinks everyone's good and worthy of attention in the end, and it makes me smile and fills me with sweetness, and makes me a little envious, there in her magic house in the woods, how she likes everybody, even me, the existentialist Taxi Driver.

And it's cool not to have to depend on anyone in your own goddam life, and I hardly do. I can live pretty much alone at times, without depending on anyone, like I did up to four months ago, going on automatic pilot. I slip my hands into my pockets and walk wherever the street takes me.

Even Martino always said he didn't need anyone.

It's too bad though, because when I go on automatic pilot the best feeling I can expect is getting trashed on Saturday night to forget another shitty week in school where nothing happened, puking just before I get home, and waking up Sunday morning with a hangover, like in a parody of some George Thorogood song.

I can *survive* on automatic pilot, but living is another thing. It's logical that ever since we tamed

the situation a bit, I can't do without her if I want
to keep it at a certain level. Same goes for her,
even if I need to hear her tell me a hundred times in
a row because I'm too scared.

When I tell Aidi, who looks real tired because
after I left she picked up a book and read till it
was finished, which wasn't long ago, she looks at me
without saying anything.

I gaze into the void a foot and a half under my
head, focus in on a generic point on the white wall,
rough, cool, as I'm about to

The only time I cried with Aidi was when Martino
died.

She squeezes my hand real tight, and when I look
back down because my neck is hurting, I can see her
brown eyes are full of tears trickling down the dark
skin of her cheeks, like in a film I've acted out so
many times in my dreams in front of a blind audience
with 3-D glasses.

I stroke her cheek with my thumb and catch an
unruly tear, then I kiss her soft salty skin ever so
slowly.

"Let's sleep a little together, Alex," she says.

We lie out on the bed, and just before falling
asleep I hear that my breath is slower than hers.
About three of hers to two of mine.

The notebook kept progressing, full of song lyrics, improvised reflections, dialogues that our pirates didn't feel like saying out loud, even a few little fairy tales, shit: the day before her departure they would seal the notebook and entrust it to Aidi's mother. "Every now and then we'll meet, when we feel like it, in the middle of the only party that never ends," a very notable narrator like Richard Bach may have written something like this in a book about distance and presence *despite* the distance. Every time old Alex read that sentence, he was taken away by so many feelings all more or less related to the idea of infinity. To tell you the truth, he felt like flying, and then, together with the aeronautic sensation, he felt a subtle anxiety that he imagined came from having to eat with utensils, from having to walk a straight line, and from all the other superstructures that took Man further away from the Infinite inside him.

In those days, our sentimental poet realized for the first time that both Antoine de Saint Exupéry and Richard Bach were airplane pilots. He also would've liked to fly, and in that way he would've experienced his first metaphorical turkey leap from Nowheresville, even if he knew perfectly well that his first real flight would occur at the same time as Aidi's, having to spend a year without her and leaving the book that was already prewritten. The same book that didn't help Martino live, our old boy thought.

Well, a cinematic shiver. The parental units finally left. They lavished him with warnings. And the Chancellor took him off to the side and told him, Look, Alex, I understand that for you all this is important but make sure not to do anything stupid, and if you want I'll leave you the keys to the office on via Ghiselli, so if you want to show Adelaide those maps it's all set, just make sure to

    a. shut off the water
    b. check to see if the door is locked
    c. leave everything like you found it

    Timeo parens et dona ferentes, I fear parental units bearing gifts. The wise guy slipped out of Grandma Pina's place with his Jollinvicta full of stuff like clothes and books, pedaling down via Saragozza around dinnertime, dark by now, avoiding two car doors that opened at the last second and howling the Cure's "Friday I'm in Love," the big hit of June which went with their story.

    "People should thank cyclists, instead they try to kill them with their fucking car doors," he said to himself. "Thank them for all the shit they don't spew out into the atmosphere, which, like they tell us in nursery school, belongs to everyone. I mean, like, the *air,* obviously."

(He played trumps with Grandma Pina at night and won a few games.)

* * *

The next morning at nine, as specified, our pirates got together in front of Alex's house. The old straightedge had the *key,* and the parental units had been dislodged for hours . . . But then, once the fucking lock to the fucking apartment got hold of the key, it wouldn't work. Aidi was as stupefied as Alex, but the phenomenon was unquestionable: the key turned once, one and a half times, but the goddam lock wouldn't click. Then candy-coated with disappointment, they packed up and bolted for the office at via Ghiselli. They spent the whole morning writing in the notebook, and at the opportune moment, in the bathroom, while our helluva guy was standing erect in front of her, she shaved him.

(The afternoon slid by with futile races, shuttling back and forth to various hardware stores.)

Fortunately, you don't become a grandmother by chance.

And after creaking across the parquet floors, rifling through her purses, inspecting her change holder and creaking back across the parquet, his mother's mother, that same night, came back into the kitchen with an orange caramel cake and a copy of the keys to his parents' house.

"Aidi?" he announced resplendently, in telephonic contact with the house by the seminary. "Tomorrow morning we can go in!"

From the magnetic archive of Mr. Alex D. The apartment is pretty spacious, with wall hangings of all kinds. My room, in the very moment I let Aidi in, is a little different from my usual room. The sun enters the room through the glass door leading onto the terrace. There are photos of the Beatles for when I'm chilling out and photos of the Sex Pistols for when I'm pissed off, and then there's Malcolm X for when I wake up at quarter after six to study because I didn't even open a book the night before, and he encourages me with his fist in the air.

Aidi brought the notebook and a couple of photo albums in her backpack. One old album from when her mom and dad were still together, right after they got married. Aidi talked about them dreamily: the golden age after the student protests, loves and plans, rents to pay and summer festivals. I envy them, even if it's over between them. In the second album there are photos of Chiara in Sicily. With cousins and friends mostly. Aidi is surprisingly close to her sister.

I don't know, I think deep down my brother likes me a lot, but he doesn't show the least bit of inter-est or admiration for what I do. My mother, in con-fidential moments, says I know perfectly well that it's not true and I just want to play the role of the misunderstood youth.

Chiara is just beautiful.

Afternoon riding the bike up and down the hills. Alone. Like a Girardengo from another time.

* * *

Then they go up to San Luca, under the longest portico in Europe. It's a Hollywood dawn, and there's no one around with it being about six in the morning and all. Camera angle from below. They climb the steps holding hands. Smiling.

From the magnetic archive of Mr. Alex D. The afternoon TV sports report says Denmark is done for, crushed under the German panzer's treads.

Aidi and me. Will we ever kiss? Will we ever make love? Will there ever be a time when we're together? And would it be better than meeting each other at quarter to six like this morning, dreaming that we're in a film together? What am I looking for? Why do I always need her to reassure me? Why do we go on with this sham of a friendship, even if it's very very special? Is it because we're so motherfucking insecure, both of us, but especially her? Would things be different if there was no America between us?

Yes.

I can't say what would happen, but the tension would definitely be lower if she wasn't leaving. Whereas now there's this feeling of the last days of Byzantium or the siege of Madrid whipping me from morning to night. Anyhow, it s a pretty remarkable thing.

I can't connect it all very well though. I woke
up too early this morning.

(Going alone to a Spanish movie without knowing any Spanish)

From the magnetic archive of Mr. Alex D. We
watched the final together. Ate spaghetti at half-
time. Denmark won. We hugged each other while the
players exchanged jerseys, and there was a certain
magic in the air. Aidi looked at me, then closed her
eyes an inch away from me. Impossible things were
happening. Then we talked about koans, Buddhist monks,
America, the Pogues, what we'll do the last night,
jealousy and distance.

I kidded around by doing imitations of her Penn-
sylvanian family that want to make her feel at home
so they organize an Italian dinner with pizza and
red wine, while the father dresses up as Pulcinella,
mangling "O Sole Mio" with a hideous falsetto.

We kissed again, a hundred times, until the
morning.

I want to sleep all afternoon. We still have
tomorrow, and the day after, and the day after
that.

(He chained the bike to the entrance gate that opened into via
Gandhi. It was the first time he'd gone to see him. There was

absolutely no one along the whole gravel path, just an enormous silence. One man was selling bunches of flowers from a stall full of tombstones. He bought some flowers, calmly, then he did what he had to do. He changed the water in the little vase, set up his new flowers, listened to that enormous silence and put the Walkman in his pocket.)

I dedicate "No Feelings" by the Sex Pistols directly from my Walkman to you, Martino. A big hug, man to man, brother to brother.

They listened to old R.E.M. and Dire Straits albums. Then, with the first words of "Tunnel of Love," Aidi sat down under the telephone table. A gesture that was hard to understand if you didn't try to attribute it to the heavy dose of mystery in the air. Old Alex would've given anything to find out what she was thinking now. At the same time, he didn't want to know.

He was confused, and he walked around the house looking at his feet.

Stress gnawed at our pirates.

But Aidi's still there, *under* the telephone table and he could've kissed her and squeezed her again. He could still keep her with him.

He gave her his orange giraffe blanket as a present. The parental units had wrapped him up in it when they took him home from the hospital

And he always used it, every winter, and now she'd sleep in it, in Pennsylvania.

The last mornings in the park they were so tense and so punctual and so sweet to each other. They were perfectly aware that this was really the end.

From the magnetic archive of Mr. Alex D.
Checklist, yes I have your address in Pennsylvania, maybe I'll send your parents a Christmas card. And one to Federico and Chiara.

A year without love and joy is looking me in the face.

But then no, she was the first not to want it, because it's not right for anyone

okay

But how the hell am I gonna deal with those afternoons when I want to see her, even for a second, maybe just passing by on my bike without her even seeing me.

For me you're more than a person, more than a friend, more than a girl, you're almost an idea, like Jonathan Livingston, but you're real too, and you're always late like I am, and you wear green sweaters even in June . . .

It's not finished, right?

No.

Promise?

Promise.

Partners on the road then.

Back to Grandma Pina's, leave the bike there, go on foot to catch the bus that'll take me to the train station.

Bolzano, one way.

Sounds like shit, right?

At the station the parental units would pick him up in their car and take me to the mountains for at least a little vacation together. On the way back they'd prick him with seven hundred thousand questions like What did you do during the week, and How's grandma, Why on earth do you keep cutting your hair that way, ad nauseam, and he'd have a headache and

Aidi would be gone.

Theirs is a story that would never work in the movies. Fortunately.

Too little sex.

But as old Holden Caulfield would say, If there's one thing I hate, it's the movies. Sort of, I guess. Anyway, don't even mention them

looking at him with those fawn eyes and in the end they say good-bye in one of those typically Hollywood dawns and he goes off pushing his old skateboard across the cold asphalt. Then, snap! close-up of her crying and zap! the screen goes black with graffitilike block letters superimposed on it, and you understand this is a page from his diary. It would probably be Marky Mark in the film though. I imagine it would cost your left nut to get Marky Mark.

Right after lunch he took a notebook out and wrote *the word* three hundred and sixty-five times, a few lines apart
    one for each day of the year. He'd bring it to Aidi this afternoon. She could read it every morning in Pennsylvania and it would be like wishing her a happy day.

he sat in front of Grandma Pina and told her everything. Her eyes lit up like she'd gone back fifty-five years, writing love letters hunched over the desk in her room. In Castel San Pietro.
    Then it was time to leave.

It's the last time he pedals up the hill to the seminary. The sky is getting darker.

No place is far. If you want to be close to the one you love, maybe you're already there?

(Alex absolutely loved having his neck stroked by a girl when his hair was real short.)

They listened to the Pogues' "Sayonara," right?

In the end it was him that melted out of the embrace, to kiss her one last time before he hopped on his bike.

He takes off without even turning around. What a helluva guy!

Faster and faster with those long strides on the straightaway. Feels no fatigue.

All right. So the two pirates decided they'd go to Paris together one day—sunglasses on their faces all happy about the trip, sitting on a bench at the Gare de Lyon. I can see myself. I could do it one day.

So why the hell are his eyes like that—I mean, all glassy and watery as he's going down via Codivilla for the last time like a slightly shorter and grungier Girardengo?

What else is that madman doing, *crying*?

Not even he knows.

He sure can pedal though, just look at him from the helicopter camera. What *composure*. Not bad, eh?

Anyway, he's hardly crying. His eyes are just a little watery, from the sheer speed, of course.

Okay. It's also because that son-of-a-bitch little prince tamed the fox. And maybe because he's thinking of how a piece of the two pirates was leaving forever. You know how some sentimental cyclists think at times. Or maybe he's just thinking about how some things can only happen once in a lifetime. Well yeah, maybe they could.

He must've surely had that girl in his mind, the one who still believes almost everyone is good. She practically lives in a house in the woods and came to the airport to say good-bye to him one day. And then he thinks about that time over the phone, when he thought it was her, but it was actually her mother.

And then there's all the afternoons spent on the grass in a certain girl's garden, a half-pirate, listening to music and talking and.

Anyway, no, he's not crying. I mean shit, he's a *Girardengo . . .*

* * *

Good God, what's that flying by?

Can you see it?

Yeah sure, let the guy race, and listen to yours truly, who's always known him. If his eyes are a little watery, it's because when old Alex flies like the wind